John Griffith London (born **John Griffith Chaney**; January 12, 1876 – November 22, 1916) was an American novelist, journalist, and social activist. A pioneer in the world of commercial magazine fiction, he was one of the first writers to become a worldwide celebrity and earn a large fortune from writing. He was also an innovator in the genre that would later become known as science fiction. His most famous works include The Call of the Wild and White Fang, both set in the Klondike Gold Rush, as well as the short stories "To Build a Fire", "An Odyssey of the North", and "Love of Life". He also wrote about the South Pacific in stories such as "The Pearls of Parlay" and "The Heathen". London was part of the radical literary group "The Crowd" in San Francisco and a passionate advocate of unionization, socialism, and the rights of workers. He wrote several powerful works dealing with these topics, such as his dystopian novel The Iron Heel, his non-fiction exposé The People of the Abyss, and The War of the Classes. (Source: Wikipedia)

Literary works:
The Cruise of the Dazzler (1902)
A Daughter of the Snows (1902)
The Call of the Wild (1903)
The Kempton-Wace Letters (1903)
The Sea-Wolf (1904)
The Game (1905)
White Fang (1906)
Before Adam (1907)
The Iron Heel (1908)
Martin Eden (1909)
Burning Daylight (1910)
Adventure (1911)
The Scarlet Plague (1912)
A Son of the Sun (1912)
The Abysmal Brute (1913)
The Valley of the Moon (1913)

THE HOUSE OF PRIDE

JACK LONDON

PRINCE CLASSICS

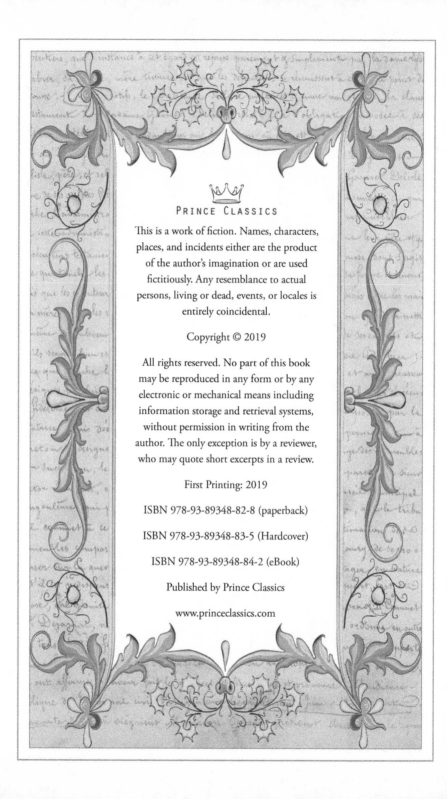

PRINCE CLASSICS

First Printing: 2019

ISBN 978-93-89348-82-8 (paperback)

ISBN 978-93-89348-83-5 (Hardcover)

ISBN 978-93-89348-84-2 (eBook)

Published by Prince Classics

www.princeclassics.com

Contents

The House of Pride

THE HOUSE OF PRIDE

Percival Ford wondered why he had come. He did not dance. He did not care much for army people. Yet he knew them all—gliding and revolving there on the broad lanai of the Seaside, the officers in their fresh-starched uniforms of white, the civilians in white and black, and the women bare of shoulders and arms. After two years in Honolulu the Twentieth was departing to its new station in Alaska, and Percival Ford, as one of the big men of the Islands, could not help knowing the officers and their women.

But between knowing and liking was a vast gulf. The army women frightened him just a little. They were in ways quite different from the women he liked best—the elderly women, the spinsters and the bespectacled maidens, and the very serious women of all ages whom he met on church and library and kindergarten committees, who came meekly to him for contributions and advice. He ruled those women by virtue of his superior mentality, his great wealth, and the high place he occupied in the commercial baronage of Hawaii. And he was not afraid of them in the least. Sex, with them, was not obtrusive. Yes, that was it. There was in them something else, or more, than the assertive grossness of life. He was fastidious; he acknowledged that to himself; and these army women, with their bare shoulders and naked arms, their straight-looking eyes, their vitality and challenging femaleness, jarred upon his sensibilities.

Nor did he get on better with the army men, who took life lightly, drinking and smoking and swearing their way through life and asserting the essential grossness of flesh no less shamelessly than their women. He was always uncomfortable in the company of the army men. They seemed uncomfortable, too. And he felt, always, that they were laughing at him up their sleeves, or pitying him, or tolerating him. Then, too, they seemed, by mere contiguity, to emphasize a lack in him, to call attention to that in them which he did not possess and which he thanked God he did not possess. Faugh! They were like their women!

In fact, Percival Ford was no more a woman's man than he was a man's man. A glance at him told the reason. He had a good constitution, never was on intimate terms with sickness, nor even mild disorders; but he lacked vitality. His was a negative organism. No blood with a ferment in it could have nourished and shaped that long and narrow face, those thin lips, lean cheeks, and the small, sharp eyes. The thatch of hair, dust-coloured, straight and sparse, advertised the niggard soil, as did the nose, thin, delicately modelled, and just hinting the suggestion of a beak. His meagre blood had denied him much of life, and permitted him to be an extremist in one thing only, which thing was righteousness. Over right conduct he pondered and agonized, and that he should do right was as necessary to his nature as loving and being loved were necessary to commoner clay.

He was sitting under the algaroba trees between the lanai and the beach. His eyes wandered over the dancers and he turned his head away and gazed seaward across the mellow-sounding surf to the Southern Cross burning low on the horizon. He was irritated by the bare shoulders and arms of the women. If he had a daughter he would never permit it, never. But his hypothesis was the sheerest abstraction. The thought process had been accompanied by no inner vision of that daughter. He did not see a daughter with arms and shoulders. Instead, he smiled at the remote contingency of marriage. He was thirty-five, and, having had no personal experience of love, he looked upon it, not as mythical, but as bestial. Anybody could marry. The Japanese and Chinese coolies, toiling on the sugar plantations and in the rice-fields, married. They invariably married at the first opportunity. It was because they were so low in the scale of life. There was nothing else for them to do. They were like the army men and women. But for him there were other and higher things. He was different from them—from all of them. He was proud of how he happened to be. He had come of no petty love-match. He had come of lofty conception of duty and of devotion to a cause. His father had not married for love. Love was a madness that had never perturbed Isaac Ford. When he answered the call to go to the heathen with the message of life, he had had no thought and no desire for marriage. In this they were alike, his father and he. But the Board of Missions was economical. With New England thrift it weighed and measured and decided that married missionaries were less expensive per capita and more efficacious. So the Board commanded Isaac Ford to marry. Furthermore, it furnished him with a wife, another zealous soul with no thought of marriage, intent only on doing the Lord's work among the heathen. They saw each other for the first time in Boston. The Board brought them together, arranged everything, and by the end of the week they were married and started on the long voyage around the Horn.

Percival Ford was proud that he had come of such a union. He had been born high, and he thought of himself as a spiritual aristocrat. And he was proud of his father. It was a passion with him. The erect, austere figure of Isaac Ford had burned itself upon his pride. On his desk was a miniature of that soldier of the Lord. In his bedroom hung the portrait of Isaac Ford, painted at the time when he had served under the Monarchy as prime minister. Not that Isaac Ford had coveted place and worldly wealth, but that, as prime minister, and, later, as banker, he had been of greater service to the missionary cause. The German crowd, and the English crowd, and all the rest of the trading crowd, had sneered at Isaac Ford as a commercial soul-saver; but he, his son, knew different. When the natives, emerging abruptly from their feudal system, with no conception of the nature and significance of property in land, were letting their broad acres slip through their fingers, it was Isaac Ford who had stepped in between the trading crowd and its prey and taken possession of fat, vast holdings. Small wonder the trading crowd did not like his memory. But he had never looked upon his enormous wealth as his own. He had considered himself God's steward. Out of the revenues he had built schools, and hospitals, and churches. Nor was it his fault that sugar, after the slump, had paid forty per cent; that the bank he founded had prospered into a railroad; and that, among other things, fifty thousand acres of Oahu pasture land, which he had bought for a dollar an acre, grew eight tons of sugar to the acre every eighteen months. No, in all truth, Isaac Ford was an heroic figure, fit, so Percival Ford thought privately, to stand beside the statue of Kamehameha I. in front of the Judiciary Building. Isaac Ford was gone, but he, his son, carried on the good work at least as inflexibly if not as masterfully.

He turned his eyes back to the lanai. What was the difference, he asked himself, between the shameless, grass-girdled hula dances and the decolleté dances of the women of his own race? Was there an essential difference? or was it a matter of degree?

As he pondered the problem a hand rested on his shoulder.

"Hello, Ford, what are you doing here? Isn't this a bit festive?"

"I try to be lenient, Dr. Kennedy, even as I look on," Percival Ford answered gravely. "Won't you sit down?"

Dr. Kennedy sat down, clapping his palms sharply. A white-clad Japanese servant answered swiftly.

Scotch and soda was Kennedy's order; then, turning to the other, he said:—

"Of course, I don't ask you."

"But I will take something," Ford said firmly. The doctor's eyes showed surprise, and the servant waited. "Boy, a lemonade, please."

The doctor laughed at it heartily, as a joke on himself, and glanced at the musicians under the hau tree.

"Why, it's the Aloha Orchestra," he said. "I thought they were with the Hawaiian Hotel on Tuesday nights. Some rumpus, I guess."

His eyes paused for a moment, and dwelt upon the one who was playing a guitar and singing a Hawaiian song to the accompaniment of all the instruments.

His face became grave as he looked at the singer, and it was still grave as he turned it to his companion.

"Look here, Ford, isn't it time you let up on Joe Garland? I understand you are in opposition to the Promotion Committee's sending him to the States on this surf-board proposition, and I've been wanting to speak to you about it. I should have thought you'd be glad to get him out of the country. It would be a good way to end your persecution of him."

"Persecution?" Percival Ford's eyebrows lifted interrogatively.

"Call it by any name you please," Kennedy went on. "You've hounded that poor devil for years. It's not his fault. Even you will admit that."

"Not his fault?" Percival Ford's thin lips drew tightly together for the moment. "Joe Garland is dissolute and idle. He has always been a wastrel, a profligate."

"But that's no reason you should keep on after him the way you do. I've watched you from the beginning. The first thing you did when you returned from college and found him working on the plantation as outside luna was to fire him—you with your millions, and he with his sixty dollars a month."

"Not the first thing," Percival Ford said judicially, in a tone he was accustomed to use in committee meetings. "I gave him his warning. The superintendent said he was a capable luna. I had no objection to him on that ground. It was what he did outside working hours. He undid my work faster than I could build it up. Of what use were the Sunday schools, the night schools, and the sewing classes, when in the evenings there was Joe Garland with his infernal and eternal tum-tumming of guitar and ukulele, his strong drink, and his hula dancing? After I warned him, I came upon him—I shall never forget it—came upon him, down at the cabins. It was evening. I could hear the hula songs before I saw the scene. And when I did see it, there were the girls, shameless in the moonlight and dancing—the girls upon whom I had worked to teach clean living and right conduct. And there were three girls there, I remember, just graduated from the mission school. Of course I discharged Joe Garland. I know it was the same at Hilo. People said I went out of my way when I persuaded Mason and Fitch to discharge him. But it was the missionaries who requested me to do so. He was undoing their work by his reprehensible example."

"Afterwards, when he got on the railroad, your railroad, he was discharged without cause," Kennedy challenged.

"Not so," was the quick answer. "I had him into my private office and talked with him for half an hour."

"You discharged him for inefficiency?"

"For immoral living, if you please."

Dr. Kennedy laughed with a grating sound. "Who the devil gave it to you to be judge and jury? Does landlordism give you control of the immortal souls of those that toil for you? I have been your physician. Am I to expect tomorrow your ukase that I give up Scotch and soda or your patronage? Bah! Ford, you take life too seriously. Besides, when Joe got into that smuggling scrape (he wasn't in your employ, either), and he sent word to you, asked you to pay his fine, you left him to do his six months' hard labour on the reef. Don't forget, you left Joe Garland in the lurch that time. You threw him down, hard; and yet I remember the first day you came to school—we boarded, you were only a day scholar—you had to be initiated. Three times under in the swimming tank—you remember, it was the regular dose every new boy got. And you held back. You denied that you could swim. You were frightened, hysterical—"

"Yes, I know," Percival Ford said slowly. "I was frightened. And it was a lie, for I could swim . . . And I was frightened."

"And you remember who fought for you? who lied for you harder than you could lie, and swore he knew you couldn't swim? Who jumped into the tank and pulled you out after the first under and was nearly drowned for it by the other boys, who had discovered by that time that you could swim?"

"Of course I know," the other rejoined coldly. "But a generous act as a boy does not excuse a lifetime of wrong living."

"He has never done wrong to you?—personally and directly, I mean?"

"No," was Percival Ford's answer. "That is what makes my position impregnable. I have no personal spite against him. He is bad, that is all. His life is bad—"

"Which is another way of saying that he does not agree with you in the way life should be lived," the doctor interrupted.

"Have it that way. It is immaterial. He is an idler—"

"With reason," was the interruption, "considering the jobs out of which you have knocked him."

"He is immoral—"

"Oh, hold on now, Ford. Don't go harping on that. You are pure New England stock. Joe Garland is half Kanaka. Your blood is thin. His is warm. Life is one thing to you, another thing to him. He laughs and sings and dances through life, genial, unselfish, childlike, everybody's friend. You go through life like a perambulating prayer-wheel, a friend of nobody but the righteous, and the righteous are those who agree with you as to what is right. And after all, who shall say? You live like an anchorite. Joe Garland lives like a good fellow. Who has extracted the most from life? We are paid to live, you know. When the wages are too meagre we throw up the job, which is the cause, believe me, of all rational suicide. Joe Garland would starve to death on the wages you get from life. You see, he is made differently. So would you starve on his wages, which are singing, and love—"

"Lust, if you will pardon me," was the interruption.

Dr. Kennedy smiled.

"Love, to you, is a word of four letters and a definition which you have extracted from the dictionary. But love, real love, dewy and palpitant and tender, you do not know. If God made you and me, and men and women, believe me He made love, too. But to come back. It's about time you quit hounding Joe Garland. It is not worthy of you, and it is cowardly. The thing for you to do is to reach out and lend him a hand."

"Why I, any more than you?" the other demanded. "Why don't you reach him a hand?"

"I have. I'm reaching him a hand now. I'm trying to get you not to down the Promotion Committee's proposition of sending him away. I got him the job at Hilo with Mason and Fitch. I've got him half a dozen jobs, out of every one of which you drove him. But never mind that. Don't forget one thing—and a little frankness won't hurt you—it is not fair play to saddle another fault on Joe Garland; and you know that you, least of all, are the man

15

to do it. Why, man, it's not good taste. It's positively indecent."

"Now I don't follow you," Percival Ford answered. "You're up in the air with some obscure scientific theory of heredity and personal irresponsibility. But how any theory can hold Joe Garland irresponsible for his wrongdoings and at the same time hold me personally responsible for them—more responsible than any one else, including Joe Garland—is beyond me."

"It's a matter of delicacy, I suppose, or of taste, that prevents you from following me," Dr. Kennedy snapped out. "It's all very well, for the sake of society, tacitly to ignore some things, but you do more than tacitly ignore."

"What is it, pray, that I tacitly ignore!"

Dr. Kennedy was angry. A deeper red than that of constitutional Scotch and soda suffused his face, as he answered:

"Your father's son."

"Now just what do you mean?"

"Damn it, man, you can't ask me to be plainer spoken than that. But if you will, all right—Isaac Ford's son—Joe Garland—your brother."

Percival Ford sat quietly, an annoyed and shocked expression on his face. Kennedy looked at him curiously, then, as the slow minutes dragged by, became embarrassed and frightened.

"My God!" he cried finally, "you don't mean to tell me that you didn't know!"

As in answer, Percival Ford's cheeks turned slowly grey.

"It's a ghastly joke," he said; "a ghastly joke."

The doctor had got himself in hand.

"Everybody knows it," he said. "I thought you knew it. And since you don't know it, it's time you did, and I'm glad of the chance of setting you straight. Joe Garland and you are brothers—half-brothers."

"It's a lie," Ford cried. "You don't mean it. Joe Garland's mother was

16

Eliza Kunilio." (Dr. Kennedy nodded.) "I remember her well, with her duck pond and taro patch. His father was Joseph Garland, the beach-comber." (Dr. Kennedy shook his head.) "He died only two or three years ago. He used to get drunk. There's where Joe got his dissoluteness. There's the heredity for you."

"And nobody told you," Kennedy said wonderingly, after a pause.

"Dr. Kennedy, you have said something terrible, which I cannot allow to pass. You must either prove or, or . . . "

"Prove it yourself. Turn around and look at him. You've got him in profile. Look at his nose. That's Isaac Ford's. Yours is a thin edition of it. That's right. Look. The lines are fuller, but they are all there."

Percival Ford looked at the Kanaka half-breed who played under the hau tree, and it seemed, as by some illumination, that he was gazing on a wraith of himself. Feature after feature flashed up an unmistakable resemblance. Or, rather, it was he who was the wraith of that other full-muscled and generously moulded man. And his features, and that other man's features, were all reminiscent of Isaac Ford. And nobody had told him. Every line of Isaac Ford's face he knew. Miniatures, portraits, and photographs of his father were passing in review through his mind, and here and there, over and again, in the face before him, he caught resemblances and vague hints of likeness. It was devil's work that could reproduce the austere features of Isaac Ford in the loose and sensuous features before him. Once, the man turned, and for one flashing instant it seemed to Percival Ford that he saw his father, dead and gone, peering at him out of the face of Joe Garland.

"It's nothing at all," he could faintly hear Dr. Kennedy saying, "They were all mixed up in the old days. You know that. You've seen it all your life. Sailors married queens and begat princesses and all the rest of it. It was the usual thing in the Islands."

"But not with my father," Percival Ford interrupted.

"There you are." Kennedy shrugged his shoulders. "Cosmic sap and smoke of life. Old Isaac Ford was straitlaced and all the rest, and I know

17

there's no explaining it, least of all to himself. He understood it no more than you do. Smoke of life, that's all. And don't forget one thing, Ford. There was a dab of unruly blood in old Isaac Ford, and Joe Garland inherited it— all of it, smoke of life and cosmic sap; while you inherited all of old Isaac's ascetic blood. And just because your blood is cold, well-ordered, and well-disciplined, is no reason that you should frown upon Joe Garland. When Joe Garland undoes the work you do, remember that it is only old Isaac Ford on both sides, undoing with one hand what he does with the other. You are Isaac Ford's right hand, let us say; Joe Garland is his left hand."

Percival Ford made no answer, and in the silence Dr. Kennedy finished his forgotten Scotch and soda. From across the grounds an automobile hooted imperatively.

"There's the machine," Dr. Kennedy said, rising. "I've got to run. I'm sorry I've shaken you up, and at the same time I'm glad. And know one thing, Isaac Ford's dab of unruly blood was remarkably small, and Joe Garland got it all. And one other thing. If your father's left hand offend you, don't smite it off. Besides, Joe is all right. Frankly, if I could choose between you and him to live with me on a desert isle, I'd choose Joe."

Little bare-legged children ran about him, playing, on the grass; but Percival Ford did not see them. He was gazing steadily at the singer under the hau tree. He even changed his position once, to get closer. The clerk of the Seaside went by, limping with age and dragging his reluctant feet. He had lived forty years on the Islands. Percival Ford beckoned to him, and the clerk came respectfully, and wondering that he should be noticed by Percival Ford.

"John," Ford said, "I want you to give me some information. Won't you sit down?"

The clerk sat down awkwardly, stunned by the unexpected honour. He blinked at the other and mumbled, "Yes, sir, thank you."

"John, who is Joe Garland?"

The clerk stared at him, blinked, cleared his throat, and said nothing.

"Go on," Percival Ford commanded.

"Who is he?"

"You're joking me, sir," the other managed to articulate.

"I spoke to you seriously."

The clerk recoiled from him.

"You don't mean to say you don't know?" he questioned, his question in itself the answer.

"I want to know."

"Why, he's—" John broke off and looked about him helplessly. "Hadn't you better ask somebody else? Everybody thought you knew. We always thought . . . "

"Yes, go ahead."

"We always thought that that was why you had it in for him."

Photographs and miniatures of Isaac Ford were trooping through his son's brain, and ghosts of Isaac Ford seemed in the air about hint "I wish you good night, sir," he could hear the clerk saying, and he saw him beginning to limp away.

"John," he called abruptly.

John came back and stood near him, blinking and nervously moistening his lips.

"You haven't told me yet, you know."

"Oh, about Joe Garland?"

"Yes, about Joe Garland. Who is he?"

"He's your brother, sir, if I say it who shouldn't."

"Thank you, John. Good night."

"And you didn't know?" the old man queried, content to linger, now that the crucial point was past.

"Thank you, John. Good night," was the response.

"Yes, sir, thank you, sir. I think it's going to rain. Good night, sir."

Out of the clear sky, filled only with stars and moonlight, fell a rain so fine and attenuated as to resemble a vapour spray. Nobody minded it; the children played on, running bare-legged over the grass and leaping into the sand; and in a few minutes it was gone. In the south-east, Diamond Head, a black blot, sharply defined, silhouetted its crater-form against the stars. At sleepy intervals the surf flung its foam across the sands to the grass, and far out could be seen the black specks of swimmers under the moon. The voices of the singers, singing a waltz, died away; and in the silence, from somewhere under the trees, arose the laugh of a woman that was a love-cry. It startled Percival Ford, and it reminded him of Dr. Kennedy's phrase. Down by the outrigger canoes, where they lay hauled out on the sand, he saw men and women, Kanakas, reclining languorously, like lotus-eaters, the women in white holokus; and against one such holoku he saw the dark head of the steersman of the canoe resting upon the woman's shoulder. Farther down, where the strip of sand widened at the entrance to the lagoon, he saw a man and woman walking side by side. As they drew near the light lanai, he saw the woman's hand go down to her waist and disengage a girdling arm. And as they passed him, Percival Ford nodded to a captain he knew, and to a major's daughter. Smoke of life, that was it, an ample phrase. And again, from under the dark algaroba tree arose the laugh of a woman that was a love-cry; and past his chair, on the way to bed, a bare-legged youngster was led by a chiding Japanese nurse-maid. The voices of the singers broke softly and meltingly into an Hawaiian love-song, and officers and women, with encircling arms, were gliding and whirling on the lanai; and once again the woman laughed under the algaroba trees.

And Percival Ford knew only disapproval of it all. He was irritated by the love-laugh of the woman, by the steersman with pillowed head on the white holoku, by the couples that walked on the beach, by the officers and women that danced, and by the voices of the singers singing of love, and his brother singing there with them under the hau tree. The woman that laughed especially irritated him. A curious train of thought was aroused. He was Isaac Ford's son, and what had happened with Isaac Ford might happen with him. He felt in his cheeks the faint heat of a blush at the thought, and experienced a poignant sense of shame. He was appalled by what was in his blood. It was like learning suddenly that his father had been a leper and that his own blood might bear the taint of that dread disease. Isaac Ford, the austere soldier of the Lord—the old hypocrite! What difference between him and any beach-comber? The house of pride that Percival Ford had builded was tumbling about his ears.

The hours passed, the army people laughed and danced, the native orchestra played on, and Percival Ford wrestled with the abrupt and overwhelming problem that had been thrust upon him. He prayed quietly, his elbow on the table, his head bowed upon his hand, with all the appearance of any tired onlooker. Between the dances the army men and women and the civilians fluttered up to him and buzzed conventionally, and when they went back to the lanai he took up his wrestling where he had left it off.

He began to patch together his shattered ideal of Isaac Ford, and for cement he used a cunning and subtle logic. It was of the sort that is compounded in the brain laboratories of egotists, and it worked. It was incontrovertible that his father had been made of finer clay than those about him; but still, old Isaac had been only in the process of becoming, while he, Percival Ford, had become. As proof of it, he rehabilitated his father and at the same time exalted himself. His lean little ego waxed to colossal proportions. He was great enough to forgive. He glowed at the thought of it. Isaac Ford had been great, but he was greater, for he could forgive Isaac Ford and even restore him to the holy place in his memory, though the place was not quite so holy as it had been. Also, he applauded Isaac Ford for having ignored the outcome of his one step aside. Very well, he, too, would ignore it.

The dance was breaking up. The orchestra had finished "Aloha Oe" and was preparing to go home. Percival Ford clapped his hands for the Japanese servant.

"You tell that man I want to see him," he said, pointing out Joe Garland. "Tell him to come here, now."

Joe Garland approached and halted respectfully several paces away, nervously fingering the guitar which he still carried. The other did not ask him to sit down.

"You are my brother," he said.

"Why, everybody knows that," was the reply, in tones of wonderment.

"Yes, so I understand," Percival Ford said dryly. "But I did not know it till this evening."

The half-brother waited uncomfortably in the silence that followed, during which Percival Ford coolly considered his next utterance.

"You remember that first time I came to school and the boys ducked me?" he asked. "Why did you take my part?"

The half-brother smiled bashfully.

"Because you knew?"

"Yes, that was why."

"But I didn't know," Percival Ford said in the same dry fashion.

"Yes," the other said.

Another silence fell. Servants were beginning to put out the lights on the lanai.

"You know . . . now," the half-brother said simply.

Percival Ford frowned. Then he looked the other over with a considering eye.

"How much will you take to leave the Islands and never come back?" he demanded.

"And never come back?" Joe Garland faltered. "It is the only land I know. Other lands are cold. I do not know other lands. I have many friends here. In other lands there would not be one voice to say, 'Aloha, Joe, my boy.'"

"I said never to come back," Percival Ford reiterated. "The Alameda sails tomorrow for San Francisco."

Joe Garland was bewildered.

"But why?" he asked. "You know now that we are brothers."

"That is why," was the retort. "As you said yourself, everybody knows. I will make it worth your while."

All awkwardness and embarrassment disappeared from Joe Garland. Birth and station were bridged and reversed.

"You want me to go?" he demanded.

"I want you to go and never come back," Percival Ford answered.

And in that moment, flashing and fleeting, it was given him to see his brother tower above him like a mountain, and to feel himself dwindle and dwarf to microscopic insignificance. But it is not well for one to see himself truly, nor can one so see himself for long and live; and only for that flashing moment did Percival Ford see himself and his brother in true perspective. The next moment he was mastered by his meagre and insatiable ego.

"As I said, I will make it worth your while. You will not suffer. I will pay you well."

"All right," Joe Garland said. "I'll go."

He started to turn away.

"Joe," the other called. "You see my lawyer tomorrow morning. Five hundred down and two hundred a month as long as you stay away."

"You are very kind," Joe Garland answered softly. "You are too kind. And anyway, I guess I don't want your money. I go tomorrow on the Alameda."

He walked away, but did not say good-bye.

Percival Ford clapped his hands.

"Boy," he said to the Japanese, "a lemonade."

And over the lemonade he smiled long and contentedly to himself.

KOOLAU THE LEPER

"Because we are sick they take away our liberty. We have obeyed the law. We have done no wrong. And yet they would put us in prison. Molokai is a prison. That you know. Niuli, there, his sister was sent to Molokai seven years ago. He has not seen her since. Nor will he ever see her. She must stay there until she dies. This is not her will. It is not Niuli's will. It is the will of the white men who rule the land. And who are these white men?

"We know. We have it from our fathers and our fathers' fathers. They came like lambs, speaking softly. Well might they speak softly, for we were many and strong, and all the islands were ours. As I say, they spoke softly. They were of two kinds. The one kind asked our permission, our gracious permission, to preach to us the word of God. The other kind asked our permission, our gracious permission, to trade with us. That was the beginning. Today all the islands are theirs, all the land, all the cattle—everything is theirs. They that preached the word of God and they that preached the word of Rum have fore-gathered and become great chiefs. They live like kings in houses of many rooms, with multitudes of servants to care for them. They who had nothing have everything, and if you, or I, or any Kanaka be hungry, they sneer and say, 'Well, why don't you work? There are the plantations.'"

Koolau paused. He raised one hand, and with gnarled and twisted fingers lifted up the blazing wreath of hibiscus that crowned his black hair. The moonlight bathed the scene in silver. It was a night of peace, though those who sat about him and listened had all the seeming of battle-wrecks. Their faces were leonine. Here a space yawned in a face where should have been a nose, and there an arm-stump showed where a hand had rotted off. They were men and women beyond the pale, the thirty of them, for upon them had been placed the mark of the beast.

They sat, flower-garlanded, in the perfumed, luminous night, and their lips made uncouth noises and their throats rasped approval of Koolau's speech. They were creatures who once had been men and women. But they were men and women no longer. They were monsters—in face and form grotesque caricatures of everything human. They were hideously maimed and distorted, and had the seeming of creatures that had been racked in millenniums of hell. Their hands, when they possessed them, were like harpy claws. Their faces were the misfits and slips, crushed and bruised by some mad god at play in the machinery of life. Here and there were features which the mad god had smeared half away, and one woman wept scalding tears from twin pits of horror, where her eyes once had been. Some were in pain and groaned from their chests. Others coughed, making sounds like the tearing of tissue. Two were idiots, more like huge apes marred in the making, until even an ape were an angel. They mowed and gibbered in the moonlight, under crowns of drooping, golden blossoms. One, whose bloated ear-lobe flapped like a fan upon his shoulder, caught up a gorgeous flower of orange and scarlet and with it decorated the monstrous ear that flip-flapped with his every movement.

And over these things Koolau was king. And this was his kingdom,—a flower-throttled gorge, with beetling cliffs and crags, from which floated the blattings of wild goats. On three sides the grim walls rose, festooned in fantastic draperies of tropic vegetation and pierced by cave-entrances— the rocky lairs of Koolau's subjects. On the fourth side the earth fell away into a tremendous abyss, and, far below, could be seen the summits of lesser peaks and crags, at whose bases foamed and rumbled the Pacific surge. In fine weather a boat could land on the rocky beach that marked the entrance of Kalalau Valley, but the weather must be very fine. And a cool-headed mountaineer might climb from the beach to the head of Kalalau Valley, to this pocket among the peaks where Koolau ruled; but such a mountaineer must be very cool of head, and he must know the wild-goat trails as well. The marvel was that the mass of human wreckage that constituted Koolau's people should have been able to drag its helpless misery over the giddy goat-trails to this inaccessible spot.

"Brothers," Koolau began.

But one of the mowing, apelike travesties emitted a wild shriek of madness, and Koolau waited while the shrill cachination was tossed back and forth among the rocky walls and echoed distantly through the pulseless night.

"Brothers, is it not strange? Ours was the land, and behold, the land is not ours. What did these preachers of the word of God and the word of Rum give us for the land? Have you received one dollar, as much as one dollar, any one of you, for the land? Yet it is theirs, and in return they tell us we can go to work on the land, their land, and that what we produce by our toil shall be theirs. Yet in the old days we did not have to work. Also, when we are sick, they take away our freedom."

"Who brought the sickness, Koolau?" demanded Kiloliana, a lean and wiry man with a face so like a laughing faun's that one might expect to see the cloven hoofs under him. They were cloven, it was true, but the cleavages were great ulcers and livid putrefactions. Yet this was Kiloliana, the most daring climber of them all, the man who knew every goat-trail and who had led Koolau and his wretched followers into the recesses of Kalalau.

"Ay, well questioned," Koolau answered. "Because we would not work the miles of sugar-cane where once our horses pastured, they brought the Chinese slaves from overseas. And with them came the Chinese sickness— that which we suffer from and because of which they would imprison us on Molokai. We were born on Kauai. We have been to the other islands, some here and some there, to Oahu, to Maui, to Hawaii, to Honolulu. Yet always did we come back to Kauai. Why did we come back? There must be a reason. Because we love Kauai. We were born here. Here we have lived. And here shall we die—unless—unless—there be weak hearts amongst us. Such we do not want. They are fit for Molokai. And if there be such, let them not remain. Tomorrow the soldiers land on the shore. Let the weak hearts go down to them. They will be sent swiftly to Molokai. As for us, we shall stay and fight. But know that we will not die. We have rifles. You know the narrow trails where men must creep, one by one. I, alone, Koolau, who was once a cowboy on Niihau, can hold the trail against a thousand men. Here is Kapalei, who was once a judge over men and a man with honour, but who is now a hunted rat, like you and me. Hear him. He is wise."

Kapalei arose. Once he had been a judge. He had gone to college at

Punahou. He had sat at meat with lords and chiefs and the high representatives of alien powers who protected the interests of traders and missionaries. Such had been Kapalei. But now, as Koolau had said, he was a hunted rat, a creature outside the law, sunk so deep in the mire of human horror that he was above the law as well as beneath it. His face was featureless, save for gaping orifices and for the lidless eyes that burned under hairless brows.

"Let us not make trouble," he began. "We ask to be left alone. But if they do not leave us alone, then is the trouble theirs and the penalty. My fingers are gone, as you see." He held up his stumps of hands that all might see. "Yet have I the joint of one thumb left, and it can pull a trigger as firmly as did its lost neighbour in the old days. We love Kauai. Let us live here, or die here, but do not let us go to the prison of Molokai. The sickness is not ours. We have not sinned. The men who preached the word of God and the word of Rum brought the sickness with the coolie slaves who work the stolen land. I have been a judge. I know the law and the justice, and I say to you it is unjust to steal a man's land, to make that man sick with the Chinese sickness, and then to put that man in prison for life."

"Life is short, and the days are filled with pain," said Koolau. "Let us drink and dance and be happy as we can."

From one of the rocky lairs calabashes were produced and passed round. The calabashes were filled with the fierce distillation of the root of the ti-plant; and as the liquid fire coursed through them and mounted to their brains, they forgot that they had once been men and women, for they were men and women once more. The woman who wept scalding tears from open eye-pits was indeed a woman apulse with life as she plucked the strings of an ukulele and lifted her voice in a barbaric love-call such as might have come from the dark forest-depths of the primeval world. The air tingled with her cry, softly imperious and seductive. Upon a mat, timing his rhythm to the woman's song Kiloliana danced. It was unmistakable. Love danced in all his movements, and, next, dancing with him on the mat, was a woman whose heavy hips and generous breast gave the lie to her disease-corroded face. It was a dance of the living dead, for in their disintegrating bodies life still loved and longed. Ever the woman whose sightless eyes ran scalding tears chanted her love-cry, ever the dancers of love danced in the warm night, and ever the calabashes went around till in all their brains were maggots crawling of memory and desire. And with the woman on the mat danced a slender maid whose face was beautiful and unmarred, but whose twisted arms that rose and fell marked the disease's ravage. And the two idiots, gibbering and mouthing strange noises, danced apart, grotesque, fantastic, travestying love as they themselves had been travestied by life.

But the woman's love-cry broke midway, the calabashes were lowered, and the dancers ceased, as all gazed into the abyss above the sea, where a rocket flared like a wan phantom through the moonlit air.

"It is the soldiers," said Koolau. "Tomorrow there will be fighting. It is well to sleep and be prepared."

The lepers obeyed, crawling away to their lairs in the cliff, until only Koolau remained, sitting motionless in the moonlight, his rifle across his knees, as he gazed far down to the boats landing on the beach.

The far head of Kalalau Valley had been well chosen as a refuge. Except Kiloliana, who knew back-trails up the precipitous walls, no man could win to the gorge save by advancing across a knife-edged ridge. This passage was a hundred yards in length. At best, it was a scant twelve inches wide. On either side yawned the abyss. A slip, and to right or left the man would fall to his death. But once across he would find himself in an earthly paradise. A sea of vegetation laved the landscape, pouring its green billows from wall to wall, dripping from the cliff-lips in great vine-masses, and flinging a spray of ferns and air-plants in to the multitudinous crevices. During the many months of Koolau's rule, he and his followers had fought with this vegetable sea. The choking jungle, with its riot of blossoms, had been driven back from the bananas, oranges, and mangoes that grew wild. In little clearings grew the wild arrowroot; on stone terraces, filled with soil scrapings, were the taro patches and the melons; and in every open space where the sunshine penetrated were papaia trees burdened with their golden fruit.

Koolau had been driven to this refuge from the lower valley by the beach. And if he were driven from it in turn, he knew of gorges among the jumbled peaks of the inner fastnesses where he could lead his subjects and live. And now he lay with his rifle beside him, peering down through a tangled screen of foliage at the soldiers on the beach. He noted that they had large guns with them, from which the sunshine flashed as from mirrors. The knife-edged passage lay directly before him. Crawling upward along the trail that led to it he could see tiny specks of men. He knew they were not the soldiers, but the police. When they failed, then the soldiers would enter the game.

He affectionately rubbed a twisted hand along his rifle barrel and made sure that the sights were clean. He had learned to shoot as a wild-cattle hunter on Niihau, and on that island his skill as a marksman was unforgotten. As the toiling specks of men grew nearer and larger, he estimated the range, judged the deflection of the wind that swept at right angles across the line of fire, and calculated the chances of overshooting marks that were so far below his level. But he did not shoot. Not until they reached the beginning of the passage did he make his presence known. He did not disclose himself, but spoke from the thicket.

"What do you want?" he demanded.

"We want Koolau, the leper," answered the man who led the native police, himself a blue-eyed American.

"You must go back," Koolau said.

He knew the man, a deputy sheriff, for it was by him that he had been harried out of Niihau, across Kauai, to Kalalau Valley, and out of the valley to the gorge.

"Who are you?" the sheriff asked.

"I am Koolau, the leper," was the reply.

"Then come out. We want you. Dead or alive, there is a thousand dollars on your head. You cannot escape."

Koolau laughed aloud in the thicket.

"Come out!" the sheriff commanded, and was answered by silence.

He conferred with the police, and Koolau saw that they were preparing to rush him.

"Koolau," the sheriff called. "Koolau, I am coming across to get you."

"Then look first and well about you at the sun and sea and sky, for it will be the last time you behold them."

"That's all right, Koolau," the sheriff said soothingly. "I know you're a dead shot. But you won't shoot me. I have never done you any wrong."

Koolau grunted in the thicket.

"I say, you know, I've never done you any wrong, have I?" the sheriff persisted.

"You do me wrong when you try to put me in prison," was the reply. "And you do me wrong when you try for the thousand dollars on my head. If you will live, stay where you are."

"I've got to come across and get you. I'm sorry. But it is my duty."

"You will die before you get across."

The sheriff was no coward. Yet was he undecided. He gazed into the gulf on either side and ran his eyes along the knife-edge he must travel. Then he made up his mind.

"Koolau," he called.

But the thicket remained silent.

"Koolau, don't shoot. I am coming."

The sheriff turned, gave some orders to the police, then started on his perilous way. He advanced slowly. It was like walking a tight rope. He had nothing to lean upon but the air. The lava rock crumbled under his feet, and on either side the dislodged fragments pitched downward through the depths. The sun blazed upon him, and his face was wet with sweat. Still he advanced, until the halfway point was reached.

"Stop!" Koolau commanded from the thicket. "One more step and I shoot."

The sheriff halted, swaying for balance as he stood poised above the void. His face was pale, but his eyes were determined. He licked his dry lips before he spoke.

"Koolau, you won't shoot me. I know you won't."

He started once more. The bullet whirled him half about. On his face was an expression of querulous surprise as he reeled to the fall. He tried to save himself by throwing his body across the knife-edge; but at that moment he knew death. The next moment the knife-edge was vacant. Then came the rush, five policemen, in single file, with superb steadiness, running along the knife-edge. At the same instant the rest of the posse opened fire on the thicket. It was madness. Five times Koolau pulled the trigger, so rapidly that his shots constituted a rattle. Changing his position and crouching low under the bullets that were biting and singing through the bushes, he peered out. Four of the police had followed the sheriff. The fifth lay across the knife-edge still alive. On the farther side, no longer firing, were the surviving police. On the naked rock there was no hope for them. Before they could clamber down Koolau could have picked off the last man. But he did not fire, and, after a conference, one of them took off a white undershirt and waved it as a flag. Followed by another, he advanced along the knife-edge to their wounded comrade. Koolau gave no sign, but watched them slowly withdraw and become specks as they descended into the lower valley.

Two hours later, from another thicket, Koolau watched a body of police trying to make the ascent from the opposite side of the valley. He saw the wild goats flee before them as they climbed higher and higher, until he doubted his judgment and sent for Kiloliana, who crawled in beside him.

"No, there is no way," said Kiloliana.

"The goats?" Koolau questioned.

"They come over from the next valley, but they cannot pass to this. There is no way. Those men are not wiser than goats. They may fall to their deaths. Let us watch."

"They are brave men," said Koolau. "Let us watch."

Side by side they lay among the morning-glories, with the yellow blossoms of the hau dropping upon them from overhead, watching the motes of men toil upward, till the thing happened, and three of them, slipping, rolling, sliding, dashed over a cliff-lip and fell sheer half a thousand feet.

Kiloliana chuckled.

"We will be bothered no more," he said.

"They have war guns," Koolau made answer. "The soldiers have not yet spoken."

In the drowsy afternoon, most of the lepers lay in their rock dens asleep. Koolau, his rifle on his knees, fresh-cleaned and ready, dozed in the entrance to his own den. The maid with the twisted arms lay below in the thicket and kept watch on the knife-edge passage. Suddenly Koolau was startled wide awake by the sound of an explosion on the beach. The next instant the atmosphere was incredibly rent asunder. The terrible sound frightened him. It was as if all the gods had caught the envelope of the sky in their hands and were ripping it apart as a woman rips apart a sheet of cotton cloth. But it was such an immense ripping, growing swiftly nearer. Koolau glanced up apprehensively, as if expecting to see the thing. Then high up on the cliff overhead the shell burst in a fountain of black smoke. The rock was shattered, the fragments falling to the foot of the cliff.

Koolau passed his hand across his sweaty brow. He was terribly shaken. He had had no experience with shell-fire, and this was more dreadful than anything he had imagined.

"One," said Kapahei, suddenly bethinking himself to keep count.

A second and a third shell flew screaming over the top of the wall, bursting beyond view. Kapahei methodically kept the count. The lepers crowded into the open space before the caves. At first they were frightened, but as the shells continued their flight overhead the leper folk became reassured and began to admire the spectacle.

The two idiots shrieked with delight, prancing wild antics as each air-tormenting shell went by. Koolau began to recover his confidence. No damage was being done. Evidently they could not aim such large missiles at such long range with the precision of a rifle.

But a change came over the situation. The shells began to fall short. One burst below in the thicket by the knife-edge. Koolau remembered the maid who lay there on watch, and ran down to see. The smoke was still rising from the bushes when he crawled in. He was astounded. The branches were splintered and broken. Where the girl had lain was a hole in the ground. The girl herself was in shattered fragments. The shell had burst right on her.

First peering out to make sure no soldiers were attempting the passage, Koolau started back on the run for the caves. All the time the shells were moaning, whining, screaming by, and the valley was rumbling and reverberating with the explosions. As he came in sight of the caves, he saw the two idiots cavorting about, clutching each other's hands with their stumps of fingers. Even as he ran, Koolau saw a spout of black smoke rise from the ground, near to the idiots. They were flung apart bodily by the explosion. One lay motionless, but the other was dragging himself by his hands toward the cave. His legs trailed out helplessly behind him, while the blood was pouring from his body. He seemed bathed in blood, and as he crawled he cried like a little dog. The rest of the lepers, with the exception of Kapahei, had fled into the caves.

"Seventeen," said Kapahei. "Eighteen," he added.

This last shell had fairly entered into one of the caves. The explosion caused the caves to empty. But from the particular cave no one emerged. Koolau crept in through the pungent, acrid smoke. Four bodies, frightfully mangled, lay about. One of them was the sightless woman whose tears till now had never ceased.

Outside, Koolau found his people in a panic and already beginning to climb the goat-trail that led out of the gorge and on among the jumbled heights and chasms. The wounded idiot, whining feebly and dragging himself along on the ground by his hands, was trying to follow. But at the first pitch of the wall his helplessness overcame him and he fell back.

"It would be better to kill him," said Koolau to Kapahei, who still sat in the same place.

"Twenty-two," Kapahei answered. "Yes, it would be a wise thing to kill him. Twenty-three—twenty-four."

The idiot whined sharply when he saw the rifle levelled at him. Koolau hesitated, then lowered the gun.

"It is a hard thing to do," he said.

"You are a fool, twenty-six, twenty-seven," said Kapahei. "Let me show you."

He arose, and with a heavy fragment of rock in his hand, approached the wounded thing. As he lifted his arm to strike, a shell burst full upon him, relieving him of the necessity of the act and at the same time putting an end to his count.

Koolau was alone in the gorge. He watched the last of his people drag their crippled bodies over the brow of the height and disappear. Then he turned and went down to the thicket where the maid had keen killed. The shell-fire still continued, but he remained; for far below he could see the soldiers climbing up. A shell burst twenty feet away. Flattening himself into the earth, he heard the rush of the fragments above his body. A shower of hau blossoms rained upon him. He lifted his head to peer down the trail, and sighed. He was very much afraid. Bullets from rifles would not have worried him, but this shell-fire was abominable. Each time a shell shrieked by he shivered and crouched; but each time he lifted his head again to watch the trail.

At last the shells ceased. This, he reasoned, was because the soldiers were drawing near. They crept along the trail in single file, and he tried to count them until he lost track. At any rate, there were a hundred or so of them—all come after Koolau the leper. He felt a fleeting prod of pride. With war guns and rifles, police and soldiers, they came for him, and he was only one man, a crippled wreck of a man at that. They offered a thousand dollars for him, dead or alive. In all his life he had never possessed that much money. The thought was a bitter one. Kapahei had been right. He, Koolau, had done no wrong. Because the haoles wanted labour with which to work the stolen land, they had brought in the Chinese coolies, and with them had come the sickness. And now, because he had caught the sickness, he was worth a thousand dollars—but not to himself. It was his worthless carcass, rotten with disease or dead from a bursting shell, that was worth all that money.

When the soldiers reached the knife-edged passage, he was prompted to warn them. But his gaze fell upon the body of the murdered maid, and he kept silent. When six had ventured on the knife-edge, he opened fire. Nor did he cease when the knife-edge was bare. He emptied his magazine, reloaded, and emptied it again. He kept on shooting. All his wrongs were blazing in his brain, and he was in a fury of vengeance. All down the goat-trail the soldiers were firing, and though they lay flat and sought to shelter themselves in the shallow inequalities of the surface, they were exposed marks to him. Bullets whistled and thudded about him, and an occasional ricochet sang sharply through the air. One bullet ploughed a crease through his scalp, and a second burned across his shoulder-blade without breaking the skin.

It was a massacre, in which one man did the killing. The soldiers began to retreat, helping along their wounded. As Koolau picked them off he became aware of the smell of burnt meat. He glanced about him at first, and then discovered that it was his own hands. The heat of the rifle was doing it. The leprosy had destroyed most of the nerves in his hands. Though his flesh burned and he smelled it, there was no sensation.

He lay in the thicket, smiling, until he remembered the war guns. Without doubt they would open upon him again, and this time upon the very thicket from which he had inflicted the danger. Scarcely had he changed his position to a nook behind a small shoulder of the wall where he had noted that no shells fell, than the bombardment recommenced. He counted the shells. Sixty more were thrown into the gorge before the war-guns ceased. The tiny area was pitted with their explosions, until it seemed impossible that any creature could have survived. So the soldiers thought, for, under the burning afternoon sun, they climbed the goat-trail again. And again the knife-edged passage was disputed, and again they fell back to the beach.

For two days longer Koolau held the passage, though the soldiers contented themselves with flinging shells into his retreat. Then Pahau, a leper boy, came to the top of the wall at the back of the gorge and shouted down to him that Kiloliana, hunting goats that they might eat, had been killed by a fall, and that the women were frightened and knew not what to do. Koolau called the boy down and left him with a spare gun with which to guard the passage. Koolau found his people disheartened. The majority of them were too helpless to forage food for themselves under such forbidding circumstances, and all were starving. He selected two women and a man who were not too far gone with the disease, and sent them back to the gorge to bring up food and mats. The rest he cheered and consoled until even the weakest took a hand in building rough shelters for themselves.

But those he had dispatched for food did not return, and he started back for the gorge. As he came out on the brow of the wall, half a dozen rifles cracked. A bullet tore through the fleshy part of his shoulder, and his cheek was cut by a sliver of rock where a second bullet smashed against the cliff. In the moment that this happened, and he leaped back, he saw that the gorge was alive with soldiers. His own people had betrayed him. The shell-fire had been too terrible, and they had preferred the prison of Molokai.

Koolau dropped back and unslung one of his heavy cartridge-belts. Lying among the rocks, he allowed the head and shoulders of the first soldier to rise clearly into view before pulling trigger. Twice this happened, and then, after some delay, in place of a head and shoulders a white flag was thrust above the edge of the wall.

"What do you want?" he demanded.

"I want you, if you are Koolau the leper," came the answer.

Koolau forgot where he was, forgot everything, as he lay and marvelled at the strange persistence of these haoles who would have their will though the sky fell in. Aye, they would have their will over all men and all things, even though they died in getting it. He could not but admire them, too, what of that will in them that was stronger than life and that bent all things to their bidding. He was convinced of the hopelessness of his struggle. There was no gainsaying that terrible will of the haoles. Though he killed a thousand, yet would they rise like the sands of the sea and come upon him, ever more and more. They never knew when they were beaten. That was their fault and their virtue. It was where his own kind lacked. He could see, now, how the handful of the preachers of God and the preachers of Rum had conquered the land. It was because—

"Well, what have you got to say? Will you come with me?"

It was he voice of the invisible man under the white flag. There he was, like any haole, driving straight toward the end determined.

"Let us talk," said Koolau.

The man's head and shoulders arose, then his whole body. He was a smooth-faced, blue-eyed youngster of twenty-five, slender and natty in his captain's uniform. He advanced until halted, then seated himself a dozen feet away.

"You are a brave man," said Koolau wonderingly. "I could kill you like a fly."

"No, you couldn't," was the answer.

"Why not?"

"Because you are a man, Koolau, though a bad one. I know your story. You kill fairly."

Koolau grunted, but was secretly pleased.

"What have you done with my people?" he demanded. "The boy, the two women, and the man?"

"They gave themselves up, as I have now come for you to do."

Koolau laughed incredulously.

"I am a free man," he announced. "I have done no wrong. All I ask is to be left alone. I have lived free, and I shall die free. I will never give myself up."

"Then your people are wiser than you," answered the young captain. "Look—they are coming now."

Koolau turned and watched the remnant of his band approach. Groaning and sighing, a ghastly procession, it dragged its wretchedness past. It was given to Koolau to taste a deeper bitterness, for they hurled imprecations and insults at him as they went by; and the panting hag who brought up the rear halted, and with skinny, harpy-claws extended, shaking her snarling death's head from side to side, she laid a curse upon him. One by one they dropped over the lip-edge and surrendered to the hiding soldiers.

"You can go now," said Koolau to the captain. "I will never give myself up. That is my last word. Good-bye."

The captain slipped over the cliff to his soldiers. The next moment, and without a flag of truce, he hoisted his hat on his scabbard, and Koolau's bullet tore through it. That afternoon they shelled him out from the beach, and as he retreated into the high inaccessible pockets beyond, the soldiers followed him.

For six weeks they hunted him from pocket to pocket, over the volcanic peaks and along the goat-trails. When he hid in the lantana jungle, they formed lines of beaters, and through lantana jungle and guava scrub they drove him like a rabbit. But ever he turned and doubled and eluded. There was no cornering him. When pressed too closely, his sure rifle held them back and they carried their wounded down the goat-trails to the beach. There were times when they did the shooting as his brown body showed for a moment through the underbrush. Once, five of them caught him on an exposed goat-trail between pockets. They emptied their rifles at him as he limped and climbed along his dizzy way. Afterwards they found bloodstains and knew that he was wounded. At the end of six weeks they gave up. The soldiers and police returned to Honolulu, and Kalalau Valley was left to him for his own, though head-hunters ventured after him from time to time and to their own undoing.

Two years later, and for the last time, Koolau crawled into a thicket and lay down among the ti-leaves and wild ginger blossoms. Free he had lived, and free he was dying. A slight drizzle of rain began to fall, and he drew a ragged blanket about the distorted wreck of his limbs. His body was covered with an oilskin coat. Across his chest he laid his Mauser rifle, lingering affectionately for a moment to wipe the dampness from the barrel. The hand with which he wiped had no fingers left upon it with which to pull the trigger.

He closed his eyes, for, from the weakness in his body and the fuzzy turmoil in his brain, he knew that his end was near. Like a wild animal he had crept into hiding to die. Half-conscious, aimless and wandering, he lived back in his life to his early manhood on Niihau. As life faded and the drip of the rain grew dim in his ears it seemed to him that he was once more in the thick of the horse-breaking, with raw colts rearing and bucking under him, his stirrups tied together beneath, or charging madly about the breaking corral and driving the helping cowboys over the rails. The next instant, and with seeming naturalness, he found himself pursuing the wild bulls of the upland pastures, roping them and leading them down to the valleys. Again the sweat and dust of the branding pen stung his eyes and bit his nostrils.

All his lusty, whole-bodied youth was his, until the sharp pangs of impending dissolution brought him back. He lifted his monstrous hands and gazed at them in wonder. But how? Why? Why should the wholeness of that wild youth of his change to this? Then he remembered, and once again, and for a moment, he was Koolau, the leper. His eyelids fluttered wearily down and the drip of the rain ceased in his ears. A prolonged trembling set up in his body. This, too, ceased. He half-lifted his head, but it fell back. Then his eyes opened, and did not close. His last thought was of his Mauser, and he pressed it against his chest with his folded, fingerless hands.

GOOD-BYE, JACK

Hawaii is a queer place. Everything socially is what I may call topsy-turvy. Not but what things are correct. They are almost too much so. But still things are sort of upside down. The most ultra-exclusive set there is the "Missionary Crowd." It comes with rather a shock to learn that in Hawaii the obscure martyrdom-seeking missionary sits at the head of the table of the moneyed aristocracy. But it is true. The humble New Englanders who came out in the third decade of the nineteenth century, came for the lofty purpose of teaching the kanakas the true religion, the worship of the one only genuine and undeniable God. So well did they succeed in this, and also in civilizing the kanaka, that by the second or third generation he was practically extinct. This being the fruit of the seed of the Gospel, the fruit of the seed of the missionaries (the sons and the grandsons) was the possession of the islands themselves,—of the land, the ports, the town sites, and the sugar plantations: The missionary who came to give the bread of life remained to gobble up the whole heathen feast.

But that is not the Hawaiian queerness I started out to tell. Only one cannot speak of things Hawaiian without mentioning the missionaries. There is Jack Kersdale, the man I wanted to tell about; he came of missionary stock. That is, on his grandmother's side. His grandfather was old Benjamin Kersdale, a Yankee trader, who got his start for a million in the old days by selling cheap whiskey and square-face gin. There's another queer thing. The old missionaries and old traders were mortal enemies. You see, their interests conflicted. But their children made it up by intermarrying and dividing the island between them.

Life in Hawaii is a song. That's the way Stoddard put it in his "Hawaii Noi":—

"Thy life is music—Fate the notes prolong!

Each isle a stanza, and the whole a song."

And he was right. Flesh is golden there. The native women are sun-ripe Junos, the native men bronzed Apollos. They sing, and dance, and all are flower-bejewelled and flower-crowned. And, outside the rigid "Missionary Crowd," the white men yield to the climate and the sun, and no matter how busy they may be, are prone to dance and sing and wear flowers behind their ears and in their hair. Jack Kersdale was one of these fellows. He was one of the busiest men I ever met. He was a several-times millionaire. He was a sugar-king, a coffee planter, a rubber pioneer, a cattle rancher, and a promoter of three out of every four new enterprises launched in the islands. He was a society man, a club man, a yachtsman, a bachelor, and withal as handsome a man as was ever doted upon by mammas with marriageable daughters. Incidentally, he had finished his education at Yale, and his head was crammed fuller with vital statistics and scholarly information concerning Hawaii Nei than any other islander I ever encountered. He turned off an immense amount of work, and he sang and danced and put flowers in his hair as immensely as any of the idlers. He had grit, and had fought two duels— both, political—when he was no more than a raw youth essaying his first adventures in politics. In fact, he played a most creditable and courageous part in the last revolution, when the native dynasty was overthrown; and he could not have been over sixteen at the time. I am pointing out that he was no coward, in order that you may appreciate what happens later on. I've seen him in the breaking yard at the Haleakala Ranch, conquering a four-year-old brute that for two years had defied the pick of Von Tempsky's cow-boys. And I must tell of one other thing. It was down in Kona,—or up, rather, for the Kona people scorn to live at less than a thousand feet elevation. We were all on the lanai of Doctor Goodhue's bungalow. I was talking with Dottie Fairchild when it happened. A big centipede—it was seven inches, for we measured it afterwards—fell from the rafters overhead squarely into her coiffure. I confess, the hideousness of it paralysed me. I couldn't move. My mind refused to work. There, within two feet of me, the ugly venomous devil was writhing in her hair. It threatened at any moment to fall down upon her exposed shoulders—we had just come out from dinner.

"What is it?" she asked, starting to raise her hand to her head.

"Don't!" I cried. "Don't!"

"But what is it?" she insisted, growing frightened by the fright she read in my eyes and on my stammering lips.

My exclamation attracted Kersdale's attention. He glanced our way carelessly, but in that glance took in everything. He came over to us, but without haste.

"Please don't move, Dottie," he said quietly.

He never hesitated, nor did he hurry and make a bungle of it.

"Allow me," he said.

And with one hand he caught her scarf and drew it tightly around her shoulders so that the centipede could not fall inside her bodice. With the other hand—the right—he reached into her hair, caught the repulsive abomination as near as he was able by the nape of the neck, and held it tightly between thumb and forefinger as he withdrew it from her hair. It was as horrible and heroic a sight as man could wish to see. It made my flesh crawl. The centipede, seven inches of squirming legs, writhed and twisted and dashed itself about his hand, the body twining around the fingers and the legs digging into the skin and scratching as the beast endeavoured to free itself. It bit him twice—I saw it—though he assured the ladies that he was not harmed as he dropped it upon the walk and stamped it into the gravel. But I saw him in the surgery five minutes afterwards, with Doctor Goodhue scarifying the wounds and injecting permanganate of potash. The next morning Kersdale's arm was as big as a barrel, and it was three weeks before the swelling went down.

All of which has nothing to do with my story, but which I could not avoid giving in order to show that Jack Kersdale was anything but a coward. It was the cleanest exhibition of grit I have ever seen. He never turned a hair. The smile never left his lips. And he dived with thumb and forefinger into Dottie Fairchild's hair as gaily as if it had been a box of salted almonds. Yet that was the man I was destined to see stricken with a fear a thousand times more hideous even than the fear that was mine when I saw that writhing abomination in Dottie Fairchild's hair, dangling over her eyes and the trap of her bodice.

I was interested in leprosy, and upon that, as upon every other island subject, Kersdale had encyclopedic knowledge. In fact, leprosy was one of his hobbies. He was an ardent defender of the settlement at Molokai, where all the island lepers were segregated. There was much talk and feeling among the natives, fanned by the demagogues, concerning the cruelties of Molokai, where men and women, not alone banished from friends and family, were compelled to live in perpetual imprisonment until they died. There were no reprieves, no commutations of sentences. "Abandon hope" was written over the portal of Molokai.

"I tell you they are happy there," Kersdale insisted. "And they are infinitely better off than their friends and relatives outside who have nothing the matter with them. The horrors of Molokai are all poppycock. I can take you through any hospital or any slum in any of the great cities of the world and show you a thousand times worse horrors. The living death! The creatures that once were men! Bosh! You ought to see those living deaths racing horses on the Fourth of July. Some of them own boats. One has a gasoline launch. They have nothing to do but have a good time. Food, shelter, clothes, medical attendance, everything, is theirs. They are the wards of the Territory. They have a much finer climate than Honolulu, and the scenery is magnificent. I shouldn't mind going down there myself for the rest of my days. It is a lovely spot."

So Kersdale on the joyous leper. He was not afraid of leprosy. He said so himself, and that there wasn't one chance in a million for him or any other white man to catch it, though he confessed afterward that one of his school chums, Alfred Starter, had contracted it, gone to Molokai, and there died.

"You know, in the old days," Kersdale explained, "there was no certain test for leprosy. Anything unusual or abnormal was sufficient to send a fellow to Molokai. The result was that dozens were sent there who were no more lepers than you or I. But they don't make that mistake now. The Board of Health tests are infallible. The funny thing is that when the test was discovered they immediately went down to Molokai and applied it, and they found a number who were not lepers. These were immediately deported. Happy to get away? They wailed harder at leaving the settlement than when they left Honolulu to go to it. Some refused to leave, and really had to be forced out. One of them even married a leper woman in the last stages and then wrote pathetic letters to the Board of Health, protesting against his expulsion on the ground that no one was so well able as he to take care of his poor old wife."

"What is this infallible test?" I demanded.

"The bacteriological test. There is no getting away from it. Doctor Hervey—he's our expert, you know—was the first man to apply it here. He is a wizard. He knows more about leprosy than any living man, and if a cure is ever discovered, he'll be that discoverer. As for the test, it is very simple. They have succeeded in isolating the bacillus leprae and studying it. They know it now when they see it. All they do is to snip a bit of skin from the suspect and subject it to the bacteriological test. A man without any visible symptoms may be chock full of the leprosy bacilli."

"Then you or I, for all we know," I suggested, "may be full of it now."

Kersdale shrugged his shoulders and laughed.

"Who can say? It takes seven years for it to incubate. If you have any doubts go and see Doctor Hervey. He'll just snip out a piece of your skin and let you know in a jiffy."

Later on he introduced me to Dr. Hervey, who loaded me down with Board of Health reports and pamphlets on the subject, and took me out to Kalihi, the Honolulu receiving station, where suspects were examined and confirmed lepers were held for deportation to Molokai. These deportations occurred about once a month, when, the last good-byes said, the lepers were marched on board the little steamer, the Noeau, and carried down to the settlement.

One afternoon, writing letters at the club, Jack Kersdale dropped in on me.

"Just the man I want to see," was his greeting. "I'll show you the saddest aspect of the whole situation—the lepers wailing as they depart for Molokai. The Noeau will be taking them on board in a few minutes. But let me warn you not to let your feelings be harrowed. Real as their grief is, they'd wail a whole sight harder a year hence if the Board of Health tried to take them away from Molokai. We've just time for a whiskey and soda. I've a carriage outside. It won't take us five minutes to get down to the wharf."

To the wharf we drove. Some forty sad wretches, amid their mats, blankets, and luggage of various sorts, were squatting on the stringer piece. The Noeau had just arrived and was making fast to a lighter that lay between her and the wharf. A Mr. McVeigh, the superintendent of the settlement, was overseeing the embarkation, and to him I was introduced, also to Dr. Georges, one of the Board of Health physicians whom I had already met at Kalihi. The lepers were a woebegone lot. The faces of the majority were hideous—too horrible for me to describe. But here and there I noticed fairly good-looking persons, with no apparent signs of the fell disease upon them. One, I noticed, a little white girl, not more than twelve, with blue eyes and golden hair. One cheek, however, showed the leprous bloat. On my remarking on the sadness of her alien situation among the brown-skinned afflicted ones, Doctor Georges replied:—

"Oh, I don't know. It's a happy day in her life. She comes from Kauai. Her father is a brute. And now that she has developed the disease she is going to join her mother at the settlement. Her mother was sent down three years ago—a very bad case."

"You can't always tell from appearances," Mr. McVeigh explained. "That man there, that big chap, who looks the pink of condition, with nothing the matter with him, I happen to know has a perforating ulcer in his foot and another in his shoulder-blade. Then there are others—there, see that girl's hand, the one who is smoking the cigarette. See her twisted fingers. That's the anæsthetic form. It attacks the nerves. You could cut her fingers off with a dull knife, or rub them off on a nutmeg-grater, and she would not experience the slightest sensation."

"Yes, but that fine-looking woman, there," I persisted; "surely, surely, there can't be anything the matter with her. She is too glorious and gorgeous altogether."

"A sad case," Mr. McVeigh answered over his shoulder, already turning away to walk down the wharf with Kersdale.

She was a beautiful woman, and she was pure Polynesian. From my meagre knowledge of the race and its types I could not but conclude that she had descended from old chief stock. She could not have been more than twenty-three or four. Her lines and proportions were magnificent, and she was just beginning to show the amplitude of the women of her race.

"It was a blow to all of us," Dr. Georges volunteered. "She gave herself up voluntarily, too. No one suspected. But somehow she had contracted the disease. It broke us all up, I assure you. We've kept it out of the papers, though. Nobody but us and her family knows what has become of her. In fact, if you were to ask any man in Honolulu, he'd tell you it was his impression that she was somewhere in Europe. It was at her request that we've been so quiet about it. Poor girl, she has a lot of pride."

"But who is she?" I asked. "Certainly, from the way you talk about her, she must be somebody."

"Did you ever hear of Lucy Mokunui?" he asked.

"Lucy Mokunui?" I repeated, haunted by some familiar association. I shook my head. "It seems to me I've heard the name, but I've forgotten it."

"Never heard of Lucy Mokunui! The Hawaiian nightingale! I beg your pardon. Of course you are a malahini, [1] and could not be expected to know. Well, Lucy Mokunui was the best beloved of Honolulu—of all Hawaii, for that matter."

"You say was," I interrupted.

"And I mean it. She is finished." He shrugged his shoulders pityingly. "A dozen haoles—I beg your pardon, white men—have lost their hearts to her at one time or another. And I'm not counting in the ruck. The dozen I refer to were haoles of position and prominence."

46

"She could have married the son of the Chief Justice if she'd wanted to. You think she's beautiful, eh? But you should hear her sing. Finest native woman singer in Hawaii Nei. Her throat is pure silver and melted sunshine. We adored her. She toured America first with the Royal Hawaiian Band. After that she made two more trips on her own—concert work."

"Oh!" I cried. "I remember now. I heard her two years ago at the Boston Symphony. So that is she. I recognize her now."

I was oppressed by a heavy sadness. Life was a futile thing at best. A short two years and this magnificent creature, at the summit of her magnificent success, was one of the leper squad awaiting deportation to Molokai. Henley's lines came into my mind:—

"The poor old tramp explains his poor old ulcers;

Life is, I think, a blunder and a shame."

I recoiled from my own future. If this awful fate fell to Lucy Mokunui, what might my lot not be?—or anybody's lot? I was thoroughly aware that in life we are in the midst of death—but to be in the midst of living death, to die and not be dead, to be one of that draft of creatures that once were men, aye, and women, like Lucy Mokunui, the epitome of all Polynesian charms, an artist as well, and well beloved of men—. I am afraid I must have betrayed my perturbation, for Doctor Georges hastened to assure me that they were very happy down in the settlement.

It was all too inconceivably monstrous. I could not bear to look at her. A short distance away, behind a stretched rope guarded by a policeman, were the lepers' relatives and friends. They were not allowed to come near. There were no last embraces, no kisses of farewell. They called back and forth to one another—last messages, last words of love, last reiterated instructions. And those behind the rope looked with terrible intensity. It was the last time they would behold the faces of their loved ones, for they were the living dead, being carted away in the funeral ship to the graveyard of Molokai.

Doctor Georges gave the command, and the unhappy wretches dragged themselves to their feet and under their burdens of luggage began to stagger across the lighter and aboard the steamer. It was the funeral procession. At once the wailing started from those behind the rope. It was blood-curdling; it was heart-rending. I never heard such woe, and I hope never to again. Kersdale and McVeigh were still at the other end of the wharf, talking earnestly—politics, of course, for both were head-over-heels in that particular game. When Lucy Mokunui passed me, I stole a look at her. She was beautiful. She was beautiful by our standards, as well—one of those rare blossoms that occur but once in generations. And she, of all women, was doomed to Molokai. She straight on board, and aft on the open deck where the lepers huddled by the rail, wailing now, to their dear ones on shore.

The lines were cast off, and the Noeau began to move away from the wharf. The wailing increased. Such grief and despair! I was just resolving that never again would I be a witness to the sailing of the Noeau, when McVeigh and Kersdale returned. The latter's eyes were sparkling, and his lips could not quite hide the smile of delight that was his. Evidently the politics they had talked had been satisfactory. The rope had been flung aside, and the lamenting relatives now crowded the stringer piece on either side of us.

"That's her mother," Doctor Georges whispered, indicating an old woman next to me, who was rocking back and forth and gazing at the steamer rail out of tear-blinded eyes. I noticed that Lucy Mokunui was also wailing. She stopped abruptly and gazed at Kersdale. Then she stretched forth her arms in that adorable, sensuous way that Olga Nethersole has of embracing an audience. And with arms outspread, she cried:

"Good-bye, Jack! Good-bye!"

He heard the cry, and looked. Never was a man overtaken by more crushing fear. He reeled on the stringer piece, his face went white to the roots of his hair, and he seemed to shrink and wither away inside his clothes. He threw up his hands and groaned, "My God! My God!" Then he controlled himself by a great effort.

"Good-bye, Lucy! Good-bye!" he called.

And he stood there on the wharf, waving his hands to her till the Noeau was clear away and the faces lining her after-rail were vague and indistinct.

"I thought you knew," said McVeigh, who had been regarding him curiously. "You, of all men, should have known. I thought that was why you were here."

"I know now," Kersdale answered with immense gravity. "Where's the carriage?"

He walked rapidly—half-ran—to it. I had to half-run myself to keep up with him.

"Drive to Doctor Hervey's," he told the driver. "Drive as fast as you can."

He sank down in a seat, panting and gasping. The pallor of his face had increased. His lips were compressed and the sweat was standing out on his forehead and upper lip. He seemed in some horrible agony.

"For God's sake, Martin, make those horses go!" he broke out suddenly. "Lay the whip into them!—do you hear?—lay the whip into them!"

"They'll break, sir," the driver remonstrated.

"Let them break," Kersdale answered. "I'll pay your fine and square you with the police. Put it to them. That's right. Faster! Faster!"

"And I never knew, I never knew," he muttered, sinking back in the seat and with trembling hands wiping the sweat away.

The carriage was bouncing, swaying and lurching around corners at such a wild pace as to make conversation impossible. Besides, there was nothing to say. But I could hear him muttering over and over, "And I never knew. I never knew."

ALOHA OE

Never are there such departures as from the dock at Honolulu. The great transport lay with steam up, ready to pull out. A thousand persons were on her decks; five thousand stood on the wharf. Up and down the long gangway passed native princes and princesses, sugar kings and the high officials of the Territory. Beyond, in long lines, kept in order by the native police, were the carriages and motor-cars of the Honolulu aristocracy. On the wharf the Royal Hawaiian Band played "Aloha Oe," and when it finished, a stringed orchestra of native musicians on board the transport took up the same sobbing strains, the native woman singer's voice rising birdlike above the instruments and the hubbub of departure. It was a silver reed, sounding its clear, unmistakable note in the great diapason of farewell.

Forward, on the lower deck, the rail was lined six deep with khaki-clad young boys, whose bronzed faces told of three years' campaigning under the sun. But the farewell was not for them. Nor was it for the white-clad captain on the lofty bridge, remote as the stars, gazing down upon the tumult beneath him. Nor was the farewell for the young officers farther aft, returning from the Philippines, nor for the white-faced, climate-ravaged women by their sides. Just aft the gangway, on the promenade deck, stood a score of United States Senators with their wives and daughters—the Senatorial junketing party that for a month had been dined and wined, surfeited with statistics and dragged up volcanic hill and down lava dale to behold the glories and resources of Hawaii. It was for the junketing party that the transport had called in at Honolulu, and it was to the junketing party that Honolulu was saying good-bye.

The Senators were garlanded and bedecked with flowers. Senator Jeremy Sambrooke's stout neck and portly bosom were burdened with a dozen wreaths. Out of this mass of bloom and blossom projected his head and the greater portion of his freshly sunburned and perspiring face. He thought the flowers an abomination, and as he looked out over the multitude on the wharf it was with a statistical eye that saw none of the beauty, but that peered into the labour power, the factories, the railroads, and the plantations that lay back of the multitude and which the multitude expressed. He saw resources and thought development, and he was too busy with dreams of material achievement and empire to notice his daughter at his side, talking with a young fellow in a natty summer suit and straw hat, whose eager eyes seemed only for her and never left her face. Had Senator Jeremy had eyes for his daughter, he would have seen that, in place of the young girl of fifteen he had brought to Hawaii a short month before, he was now taking away with him a woman.

Hawaii has a ripening climate, and Dorothy Sambrooke had been exposed to it under exceptionally ripening circumstances. Slender, pale, with blue eyes a trifle tired from poring over the pages of books and trying to muddle into an understanding of life—such she had been the month before. But now the eyes were warm instead of tired, the cheeks were touched with the sun, and the body gave the first hint and promise of swelling lines. During that month she had left books alone, for she had found greater joy in reading from the book of life. She had ridden horses, climbed volcanoes, and learned surf swimming. The tropics had entered into her blood, and she was aglow with the warmth and colour and sunshine. And for a month she had been in the company of a man—Stephen Knight, athlete, surf-board rider, a bronzed god of the sea who bitted the crashing breakers, leaped upon their backs, and rode them in to shore.

Dorothy Sambrooke was unaware of the change. Her consciousness was still that of a young girl, and she was surprised and troubled by Steve's conduct in this hour of saying good-bye. She had looked upon him as her playfellow, and for the month he had been her playfellow; but now he was not parting like a playfellow. He talked excitedly and disconnectedly, or was silent, by fits and starts. Sometimes he did not hear what she was saying, or if he did, failed to respond in his wonted manner. She was perturbed by the way he looked at her. She had not known before that he had such blazing eyes. There was something in his eyes that was terrifying. She could not face it, and her own eyes continually drooped before it. Yet there was something alluring about it, as well, and she continually returned to catch a glimpse of that blazing, imperious, yearning something that she had never seen in human eyes before. And she was herself strangely bewildered and excited.

The transport's huge whistle blew a deafening blast, and the flower-crowned multitude surged closer to the side of the dock. Dorothy Sambrooke's fingers were pressed to her ears; and as she made a moue of distaste at the outrage of sound, she noticed again the imperious, yearning blaze in Steve's eyes. He was not looking at her, but at her ears, delicately pink and transparent in the slanting rays of the afternoon sun. Curious and fascinated, she gazed at that strange something in his eyes until he saw that he had been caught. She saw his cheeks flush darkly and heard him utter inarticulately. He was embarrassed, and she was aware of embarrassment herself. Stewards were going about nervously begging shore-going persons to be gone. Steve put out his hand. When she felt the grip of the fingers that had gripped hers a thousand times on surf-boards and lava slopes, she heard the words of the song with a new understanding as they sobbed in the Hawaiian woman's silver throat:

"Ka halia ko aloha kai hiki mai,

Ke hone ae nei i ku'u manawa,

O oe no kan aloha

A loko e hana nei."

Steve had taught her air and words and meaning—so she had thought, till this instant; and in this instant of the last finger clasp and warm contact of palms she divined for the first time the real meaning of the song. She scarcely saw him go, nor could she note him on the crowded gangway, for she was deep in a memory maze, living over the four weeks just past, rereading events in the light of revelation.

When the Senatorial party had landed, Steve had been one of the committee of entertainment. It was he who had given them their first exhibition of surf riding, out at Waikiki Beach, paddling his narrow board seaward until he became a disappearing speck, and then, suddenly reappearing, rising like a sea-god from out of the welter of spume and churning white—rising swiftly higher and higher, shoulders and chest and loins and limbs, until he stood poised on the smoking crest of a mighty, mile-long billow, his feet buried in the flying foam, hurling beach-ward with the speed of an express train and stepping calmly ashore at their astounded feet. That had been her first glimpse of Steve. He had been the youngest man on the committee, a youth, himself, of twenty. He had not entertained by speechmaking, nor had he shone decoratively at receptions. It was in the breakers at Waikiki, in the wild cattle drive on Manna Kea, and in the breaking yard of the Haleakala Ranch that he had performed his share of the entertaining.

She had not cared for the interminable statistics and eternal speechmaking of the other members of the committee. Neither had Steve. And it was with Steve that she had stolen away from the open-air feast at Hamakua, and from Abe Louisson, the coffee planter, who had talked coffee, coffee, nothing but coffee, for two mortal hours. It was then, as they rode among the tree ferns, that Steve had taught her the words of "Aloha Oe," the song that had been sung to the visiting Senators at every village, ranch, and plantation departure.

Steve and she had been much together from the first. He had been her playfellow. She had taken possession of him while her father had been occupied in taking possession of the statistics of the island territory. She was too gentle to tyrannize over her playfellow, yet she had ruled him abjectly, except when in canoe, or on horse or surf-board, at which times he had taken charge and she had rendered obedience. And now, with this last singing of the song, as the lines were cast off and the big transport began backing slowly out from the dock, she knew that Steve was something more to her than playfellow.

Five thousand voices were singing "Aloha Oe,"—"My love be with you till we meet again,"—and in that first moment of known love she realized that she and Steve were being torn apart. When would they ever meet again? He had taught her those words himself. She remembered listening as he sang them over and over under the hau tree at Waikiki. Had it been prophecy? And she had admired his singing, had told him that he sang with such expression. She laughed aloud, hysterically, at the recollection. With such expression!—when he had been pouring his heart out in his voice. She knew now, and it was too late. Why had he not spoken? Then she realized that girls of her age did not marry. But girls of her age did marry—in Hawaii—was her instant thought. Hawaii had ripened her—Hawaii, where flesh is golden and where all women are ripe and sun-kissed.

Vainly she scanned the packed multitude on the dock. What had become of him? She felt she could pay any price for one more glimpse of him, and she almost hoped that some mortal sickness would strike the lonely captain on the bridge and delay departure. For the first time in her life she looked at her father with a calculating eye, and as she did she noted with newborn fear the lines of will and determination. It would be terrible to oppose him. And what chance would she have in such a struggle? But why had Steve not spoken? Now it was too late. Why had he not spoken under the hau tree at Waikiki?

And then, with a great sinking of the heart, it came to her that she knew why. What was it she had heard one day? Oh, yes, it was at Mrs. Stanton's tea, that afternoon when the ladies of the "Missionary Crowd" had entertained the ladies of the Senatorial party. It was Mrs. Hodgkins, the tall blonde woman, who had asked the question. The scene came back to her vividly—the broad lanai, the tropic flowers, the noiseless Asiatic attendants, the hum of the voices of the many women and the question Mrs. Hodgkins had asked in the group next to her. Mrs. Hodgkins had been away on the mainland for years, and was evidently inquiring after old island friends of her maiden days. "What has become of Susie Maydwell?" was the question she had asked. "Oh, we never see her any more; she married Willie Kupele," another island woman answered. And Senator Behrend's wife laughed and wanted to know why matrimony had affected Susie Maydwell's friendships.

"Hapa-haole," was the answer; "he was a half-caste, you know, and we of the Islands have to think about our children."

Dorothy turned to her father, resolved to put it to the test.

"Papa, if Steve ever comes to the United States, mayn't he come and see us some time?"

"Who? Steve?"

"Yes, Stephen Knight—you know him. You said good-bye to him not five minutes ago. Mayn't he, if he happens to be in the United States some time, come and see us?"

"Certainly not," Jeremy Sambrooke answered shortly. "Stephen Knight is a hapa-haole and you know what that means."

"Oh," Dorothy said faintly, while she felt a numb despair creep into her heart.

Steve was not a hapa-haole—she knew that; but she did not know that a quarter-strain of tropic sunshine streamed in his veins, and she knew that that was sufficient to put him outside the marriage pale. It was a strange world. There was the Honourable A. S. Cleghorn, who had married a dusky princess of the Kamehameha blood, yet men considered it an honour to know him, and the most exclusive women of the ultra-exclusive "Missionary Crowd" were to be seen at his afternoon teas. And there was Steve. No one had disapproved of his teaching her to ride a surf-board, nor of his leading her by the hand through the perilous places of the crater of Kilauea. He could have dinner with her and her father, dance with her, and be a member of the entertainment committee; but because there was tropic sunshine in his veins he could not marry her.

And he didn't show it. One had to be told to know. And he was so good-looking. The picture of him limned itself on her inner vision, and before she was aware she was pleasuring in the memory of the grace of his magnificent body, of his splendid shoulders, of the power in him that tossed her lightly on a horse, bore her safely through the thundering breakers, or towed her at the end of an alpenstock up the stern lava crest of the House of the Sun. There was something subtler and mysterious that she remembered, and that she was even then just beginning to understand—the aura of the male creature that is man, all man, masculine man. She came to herself with a shock of shame at the thoughts she had been thinking. Her cheeks were dyed with the hot blood which quickly receded and left them pale at the thought that she would never see him again. The stem of the transport was already out in the stream, and the promenade deck was passing abreast of the end of the dock.

"There's Steve now," her father said. "Wave good-bye to him, Dorothy."

Steve was looking up at her with eager eyes, and he saw in her face what he had not seen before. By the rush of gladness into his own face she knew that he knew. The air was throbbing with the song—

My love to you.

My love be with you till we meet again.

There was no need for speech to tell their story. About her, passengers were flinging their garlands to their friends on the dock. Steve held up his hands and his eyes pleaded. She slipped her own garland over her head, but it had become entangled in the string of Oriental pearls that Mervin, an elderly sugar king, had placed around her neck when he drove her and her father down to the steamer.

She fought with the pearls that clung to the flowers. The transport was moving steadily on. Steve was already beneath her. This was the moment. The next moment and he would be past. She sobbed, and Jeremy Sambrooke glanced at her inquiringly.

"Dorothy!" he cried sharply.

She deliberately snapped the string, and, amid a shower of pearls, the flowers fell to the waiting lover. She gazed at him until the tears blinded her and she buried her face on the shoulder of Jeremy Sambrooke, who forgot his beloved statistics in wonderment at girl babies that insisted on growing up. The crowd sang on, the song growing fainter in the distance, but still melting with the sensuous love-languor of Hawaii, the words biting into her heart like acid because of their untruth.

Aloha oe, Aloha oe, e ke onaona no ho ika lipo,

A fond embrace, ahoi ae au, until we meet again.

CHUN AH CHUN

There was nothing striking in the appearance of Chun Ah Chun. He was rather undersized, as Chinese go, and the Chinese narrow shoulders and spareness of flesh were his. The average tourist, casually glimpsing him on the streets of Honolulu, would have concluded that he was a good-natured little Chinese, probably the proprietor of a prosperous laundry or tailorshop. In so far as good nature and prosperity went, the judgment would be correct, though beneath the mark; for Ah Chun was as good-natured as he was prosperous, and of the latter no man knew a tithe the tale. It was well known that he was enormously wealthy, but in his case "enormous" was merely the symbol for the unknown.

Ah Chun had shrewd little eyes, black and beady and so very little that they were like gimlet-holes. But they were wide apart, and they sheltered under a forehead that was patently the forehead of a thinker. For Ah Chun had his problems, and had had them all his life. Not that he ever worried over them. He was essentially a philosopher, and whether as coolie, or multi-millionaire and master of many men, his poise of soul was the same. He lived always in the high equanimity of spiritual repose, undeterred by good fortune, unruffled by ill fortune. All things went well with him, whether they were blows from the overseer in the cane field or a slump in the price of sugar when he owned those cane fields himself. Thus, from the steadfast rock of his sure content he mastered problems such as are given to few men to consider, much less to a Chinese peasant.

He was precisely that—a Chinese peasant, born to labour in the fields all his days like a beast, but fated to escape from the fields like the prince in a fairy tale. Ah Chun did not remember his father, a small farmer in a district not far from Canton; nor did he remember much of his mother, who had died when he was six. But he did remember his respected uncle, Ah Kow, for him had he served as a slave from his sixth year to his twenty-fourth. It was then that he escaped by contracting himself as a coolie to labour for three years on the sugar plantations of Hawaii for fifty cents a day.

Ah Chun was observant. He perceived little details that not one man in a thousand ever noticed. Three years he worked in the field, at the end of which time he knew more about cane-growing than the overseers or even the superintendent, while the superintendent would have been astounded at the knowledge the weazened little coolie possessed of the reduction processes in the mill. But Ah Chun did not study only sugar processes. He studied to find out how men came to be owners of sugar mills and plantations. One judgment he achieved early, namely, that men did not become rich from the labour of their own hands. He knew, for he had laboured for a score of years himself. The men who grew rich did so from the labour of the hands of others. That man was richest who had the greatest number of his fellow creatures toiling for him.

So, when his term of contract was up, Ah Chun invested his savings in a small importing store, going into partnership with one, Ah Yung. The firm ultimately became the great one of "Ah Chun and Ah Yung," which handled anything from India silks and ginseng to guano islands and blackbird brigs. In the meantime, Ah Chun hired out as cook. He was a good cook, and in three years he was the highest-paid chef in Honolulu. His career was assured, and he was a fool to abandon it, as Dantin, his employer, told him; but Ah Chun knew his own mind best, and for knowing it was called a triple-fool and given a present of fifty dollars over and above the wages due him.

The firm of Ah Chun and Ah Yung was prospering. There was no need for Ah Chun longer to be a cook. There were boom times in Hawaii. Sugar was being extensively planted, and labour was needed. Ah Chun saw the chance, and went into the labour-importing business. He brought thousands of Cantonese coolies into Hawaii, and his wealth began to grow. He made investments. His beady black eyes saw bargains where other men saw bankruptcy. He bought a fish-pond for a song, which later paid five hundred per cent and was the opening wedge by which he monopolized the fish market of Honolulu. He did not talk for publication, nor figure in politics, nor play at revolutions, but he forecast events more clearly and farther ahead than did the men who engineered them. In his mind's eye he saw Honolulu a modern, electric-lighted city at a time when it straggled, unkempt and sand-tormented, over a barren reef of uplifted coral rock. So he bought land. He bought land from merchants who needed ready cash, from impecunious natives, from riotous traders' sons, from widows and orphans and the lepers deported to Molokai; and, somehow, as the years went by, the pieces of land he had bought proved to be needed for warehouses, or coffee buildings, or hotels. He leased, and rented, sold and bought, and resold again.

But there were other things as well. He put his confidence and his money into Parkinson, the renegade captain whom nobody would trust. And Parkinson sailed away on mysterious voyages in the little Vega. Parkinson was taken care of until he died, and years afterward Honolulu was astonished when the news leaked out that the Drake and Acorn guano islands had been sold to the British Phosphate Trust for three-quarters of a million. Then there were the fat, lush days of King Kalakaua, when Ah Chun paid three hundred thousand dollars for the opium licence. If he paid a third of a million for the drug monopoly, the investment was nevertheless a good one, for the dividends bought him the Kalalau Plantation, which, in turn, paid him thirty per cent for seventeen years and was ultimately sold by him for a million and a half.

It was under the Kamehamehas, long before, that he had served his own country as Chinese Consul—a position that was not altogether unlucrative; and it was under Kamehameha IV that he changed his citizenship, becoming an Hawaiian subject in order to marry Stella Allendale, herself a subject of the brown-skinned king, though more of Anglo-Saxon blood ran in her veins than of Polynesian. In fact, the random breeds in her were so attenuated that they were valued at eighths and sixteenths. In the latter proportions was the blood of her great-grandmother, Paahao—the Princess Paahao, for she came of the royal line. Stella Allendale's great-grandfather had been a Captain Blunt, an English adventurer who took service under Kamehameha I and was made a tabu chief himself. Her grandfather had been a New Bedford whaling captain, while through her own father had been introduced a remote blend of Italian and Portuguese which had been grafted upon his own English stock. Legally a Hawaiian, Ah Chun's spouse was more of any one of three other nationalities.

And into this conglomerate of the races, Ah Chun introduced the Mongolian mixture. Thus, his children by Mrs. Ah Chun were one thirty-second Polynesian, one-sixteenth Italian, one sixteenth Portuguese, one-half Chinese, and eleven thirty-seconds English and American. It might well be that Ah Chun would have refrained from matrimony could he have foreseen the wonderful family that was to spring from this union. It was wonderful in many ways. First, there was its size. There were fifteen sons and daughters, mostly daughters. The sons had come first, three of them, and then had followed, in unswerving sequence, a round dozen of girls. The blend of the race was excellent. Not alone fruitful did it prove, for the progeny, without exception, was healthy and without blemish. But the most amazing thing about the family was its beauty. All the girls were beautiful—delicately, ethereally beautiful. Mamma Ah Chun's rotund lines seemed to modify papa Ah Chun's lean angles, so that the daughters were willowy without being lathy, round-muscled without being chubby. In every feature of every face were haunting reminiscences of Asia, all manipulated over and disguised by Old England, New England, and South of Europe. No observer, without information, would have guessed, the heavy Chinese strain in their veins; nor could any observer, after being informed, fail to note immediately the Chinese traces.

As beauties, the Ah Chun girls were something new. Nothing like them had been seen before. They resembled nothing so much as they resembled one another, and yet each girl was sharply individual. There was no mistaking one for another. On the other hand, Maud, who was blue-eyed and yellow-haired, would remind one instantly of Henrietta, an olive brunette with large, languishing dark eyes and hair that was blue-black. The hint of resemblance that ran through them all, reconciling every differentiation, was Ah Chun's contribution. He had furnished the groundwork upon which had been traced the blended patterns of the races. He had furnished the slim-boned Chinese frame, upon which had been builded the delicacies and subtleties of Saxon, Latin, and Polynesian flesh.

Mrs. Ah Chun had ideas of her own to which Ah Chun gave credence, though never permitting them expression when they conflicted with his own philosophic calm. She had been used all her life to living in European fashion. Very well. Ah Chun gave her a European mansion. Later, as his sons and daughters grew able to advise, he built a bungalow, a spacious, rambling affair, as unpretentious as it was magnificent. Also, as time went by, there arose a mountain house on Tantalus, to which the family could flee when the "sick wind" blew from the south. And at Waikiki he built a beach residence on an extensive site so well chosen that later on, when the United States government condemned it for fortification purposes, an immense sum accompanied the condemnation. In all his houses were billiard and smoking rooms and guest rooms galore, for Ah Chun's wonderful progeny was given to lavish entertainment. The furnishing was extravagantly simple. Kings' ransoms were expended without display—thanks to the educated tastes of the progeny.

Ah Chun had been liberal in the matter of education. "Never mind expense," he had argued in the old days with Parkinson when that slack mariner could see no reason for making the Vega seaworthy; "you sail the schooner, I pay the bills." And so with his sons and daughters. It had been for them to get the education and never mind the expense. Harold, the eldest-born, had gone to Harvard and Oxford; Albert and Charles had gone through Yale in the same classes. And the daughters, from the eldest down, had undergone their preparation at Mills Seminary in California and passed on to Vassar, Wellesley, or Bryn Mawr. Several, having so desired, had had the finishing touches put on in Europe. And from all the world Ah Chun's sons and daughters returned to him to suggest and advise in the garnishment of the chaste magnificence of his residences. Ah Chun himself preferred the voluptuous glitter of Oriental display; but he was a philosopher, and he clearly saw that his children's tastes were correct according to Western standards.

Of course, his children were not known as the Ah Chun children. As he had evolved from a coolie labourer to a multi-millionaire, so had his name evolved. Mamma Ah Chun had spelled it A'Chun, but her wiser offspring had elided the apostrophe and spelled it Achun. Ah Chun did not object. The spelling of his name interfered no whit with his comfort nor his philosophic

61

calm. Besides, he was not proud. But when his children arose to the height of a starched shirt, a stiff collar, and a frock coat, they did interfere with his comfort and calm. Ah Chun would have none of it. He preferred the loose-flowing robes of China, and neither could they cajole nor bully him into making the change. They tried both courses, and in the latter one failed especially disastrously. They had not been to America for nothing. They had learned the virtues of the boycott as employed by organized labour, and he, their father, Chun Ah Chun, they boycotted in his own house, Mamma Achun aiding and abetting. But Ah Chun himself, while unversed in Western culture, was thoroughly conversant with Western labour conditions. An extensive employer of labour himself, he knew how to cope with its tactics. Promptly he imposed a lockout on his rebellious progeny and erring spouse. He discharged his scores of servants, locked up his stables, closed his houses, and went to live in the Royal Hawaiian Hotel, in which enterprise he happened to be the heaviest stockholder. The family fluttered distractedly on visits about with friends, while Ah Chun calmly managed his many affairs, smoked his long pipe with the tiny silver bowl, and pondered the problem of his wonderful progeny.

This problem did not disturb his calm. He knew in his philosopher's soul that when it was ripe he would solve it. In the meantime he enforced the lesson that complacent as he might be, he was nevertheless the absolute dictator of the Achun destinies. The family held out for a week, then returned, along with Ah Chun and the many servants, to occupy the bungalow once more. And thereafter no question was raised when Ah Chun elected to enter his brilliant drawing-room in blue silk robe, wadded slippers, and black silk skull-cap with red button peak, or when he chose to draw at his slender-stemmed silver-bowled pipe among the cigarette-and cigar-smoking officers and civilians on the broad verandas or in the smoking room.

Ah Chun occupied a unique position in Honolulu. Though he did not appear in society, he was eligible anywhere. Except among the Chinese merchants of the city, he never went out; but he received, and he always was the centre of his household and the head of his table. Himself peasant, born Chinese, he presided over an atmosphere of culture and refinement second to none in all the islands. Nor were there any in all the islands too proud to cross his threshold and enjoy his hospitality. First of all, the Achun bungalow was of irreproachable tone. Next, Ah Chun was a power. And finally, Ah Chun was a moral paragon and an honest business man. Despite the fact that business morality was higher than on the mainland, Ah Chun outshone the business men of Honolulu in the scrupulous rigidity of his honesty. It was a saying that his word was as good as his bond. His signature was never needed to bind him. He never broke his word. Twenty years after Hotchkiss, of Hotchkiss, Morterson Company, died, they found among mislaid papers a memorandum of a loan of thirty thousand dollars to Ah Chun. It had been incurred when Ah Chun was Privy Councillor to Kamehameha II. In the bustle and confusion of those heyday, money-making times, the affair had slipped Ah Chun's mind. There was no note, no legal claim against him, but he settled in full with the Hotchkiss' Estate, voluntarily paying a compound interest that dwarfed the principal. Likewise, when he verbally guaranteed the disastrous Kakiku Ditch Scheme, at a time when the least sanguine did not dream a guarantee necessary—"Signed his cheque for two hundred thousand without a quiver, gentlemen, without a quiver," was the report of the secretary of the defunct enterprise, who had been sent on the forlorn hope of finding out Ah Chun's intentions. And on top of the many similar actions that were true of his word, there was scarcely a man of repute in the islands that at one time or another had not experienced the helping financial hand of Ah Chun.

So it was that Honolulu watched his wonderful family grow up into a perplexing problem and secretly sympathized with him, for it was beyond any of them to imagine what he was going to do with it. But Ah Chun saw the problem more clearly than they. No one knew as he knew the extent to which he was an alien in his family. His own family did not guess it. He saw that there was no place for him amongst this marvellous seed of his loins, and he looked forward to his declining years and knew that he would grow more and more alien. He did not understand his children. Their conversation was of things that did not interest him and about which he knew nothing. The culture of the West had passed him by. He was Asiatic to the last fibre, which meant that he was heathen. Their Christianity was to him so much nonsense. But all this he would have ignored as extraneous and irrelevant, could he have

63

but understood the young people themselves. When Maud, for instance, told him that the housekeeping bills for the month were thirty thousand—that he understood, as he understood Albert's request for five thousand with which to buy the schooner yacht Muriel and become a member of the Hawaiian Yacht Club. But it was their remoter, complicated desires and mental processes that obfuscated him. He was not slow in learning that the mind of each son and daughter was a secret labyrinth which he could never hope to tread. Always he came upon the wall that divides East from West. Their souls were inaccessible to him, and by the same token he knew that his soul was inaccessible to them.

Besides, as the years came upon him, he found himself harking back more and more to his own kind. The reeking smells of the Chinese quarter were spicy to him. He sniffed them with satisfaction as he passed along the street, for in his mind they carried him back to the narrow tortuous alleys of Canton swarming with life and movement. He regretted that he had cut off his queue to please Stella Allendale in the prenuptial days, and he seriously considered the advisability of shaving his crown and growing a new one. The dishes his highly paid chef concocted for him failed to tickle his reminiscent palate in the way that the weird messes did in the stuffy restaurant down in the Chinese quarter. He enjoyed vastly more a half-hour's smoke and chat with two or three Chinese chums, than to preside at the lavish and elegant dinners for which his bungalow was famed, where the pick of the Americans and Europeans sat at the long table, men and women on equality, the women with jewels that blazed in the subdued light against white necks and arms, the men in evening dress, and all chattering and laughing over topics and witticisms that, while they were not exactly Greek to him, did not interest him nor entertain.

But it was not merely his alienness and his growing desire to return to his Chinese flesh-pots that constituted the problem. There was also his wealth. He had looked forward to a placid old age. He had worked hard. His reward should have been peace and repose. But he knew that with his immense fortune peace and repose could not possibly be his. Already there were signs and omens. He had seen similar troubles before. There was his old employer, Dantin, whose children had wrested from him, by due process of law, the management of his property, having the Court appoint guardians to administer it for him. Ah Chun knew, and knew thoroughly well, that had Dantin been a poor man, it would have been found that he could quite rationally manage his own affairs. And old Dantin had had only three children and half a million, while he, Chun Ah Chun, had fifteen children and no one but himself knew how many millions.

"Our daughters are beautiful women," he said to his wife, one evening. "There are many young men. The house is always full of young men. My cigar bills are very heavy. Why are there no marriages?"

Mamma Achun shrugged her shoulders and waited.

"Women are women and men are men—it is strange there are no marriages. Perhaps the young men do not like our daughters."

"Ah, they like them well enough," Mamma Chun answered; "but you see, they cannot forget that you are your daughters' father."

"Yet you forgot who my father was," Ah Chun said gravely. "All you asked was for me to cut off my queue."

"The young men are more particular than I was, I fancy."

"What is the greatest thing in the world?" Ah Chun demanded with abrupt irrelevance.

Mamma Achun pondered for a moment, then replied: "God."

He nodded. "There are gods and gods. Some are paper, some are wood, some are bronze. I use a small one in the office for a paper-weight. In the Bishop Museum are many gods of coral rock and lava stone."

"But there is only one God," she announced decisively, stiffening her ample frame argumentatively.

Ah Chun noted the danger signal and sheered off.

"What is greater than God, then?" he asked. "I will tell you. It is money. In my time I have had dealings with Jews and Christians, Mohammedans and

65

Buddhists, and with little black men from the Solomons and New Guinea who carried their god about them, wrapped in oiled paper. They possessed various gods, these men, but they all worshipped money. There is that Captain Higginson. He seems to like Henrietta."

"He will never marry her," retorted Mamma Achun. "He will be an admiral before he dies—"

"A rear-admiral," Ah Chun interpolated.

"Yes, I know. That is the way they retire."

"His family in the United States is a high one. They would not like it if he married . . . if he did not marry an American girl."

Ah Chun knocked the ashes out of his pipe, thoughtfully refilling the silver bowl with a tiny pleget of tobacco. He lighted it and smoked it out before he spoke.

"Henrietta is the oldest girl. The day she marries I will give her three hundred thousand dollars. That will fetch that Captain Higginson and his high family along with him. Let the word go out to him. I leave it to you."

And Ah Chun sat and smoked on, and in the curling smoke-wreaths he saw take shape the face and figure of Toy Shuey—Toy Shuey, the maid of all work in his uncle's house in the Cantonese village, whose work was never done and who received for a whole year's work one dollar. And he saw his youthful self arise in the curling smoke, his youthful self who had toiled eighteen years in his uncle's field for little more. And now he, Ah Chun, the peasant, dowered his daughter with three hundred thousand years of such toil. And she was but one daughter of a dozen. He was not elated at the thought. It struck him that it was a funny, whimsical world, and he chuckled aloud and startled Mamma Achun from a revery which he knew lay deep in the hidden crypts of her being where he had never penetrated.

But Ah Chun's word went forth, as a whisper, and Captain Higginson forgot his rear-admiralship and his high family and took to wife three hundred thousand dollars and a refined and cultured girl who was one thirty-second

Polynesian, one-sixteenth Italian, one-sixteenth Portuguese, eleven thirty-seconds English and Yankee, and one-half Chinese.

Ah Chun's munificence had its effect. His daughters became suddenly eligible and desirable. Clara was the next, but when the Secretary of the Territory formally proposed for her, Ah Chun informed him that he must wait his turn, that Maud was the oldest and that she must be married first. It was shrewd policy. The whole family was made vitally interested in marrying off Maud, which it did in three months, to Ned Humphreys, the United States immigration commissioner. Both he and Maud complained, for the dowry was only two hundred thousand. Ah Chun explained that his initial generosity had been to break the ice, and that after that his daughters could not expect otherwise than to go more cheaply.

Clara followed Maud, and thereafter, for a space of two years; there was a continuous round of weddings in the bungalow. In the meantime Ah Chun had not been idle. Investment after investment was called in. He sold out his interests in a score of enterprises, and step by step, so as not to cause a slump in the market, he disposed of his large holdings in real estate. Toward the last he did precipitate a slump and sold at sacrifice. What caused this haste were the squalls he saw already rising above the horizon. By the time Lucille was married, echoes of bickerings and jealousies were already rumbling in his ears. The air was thick with schemes and counter-schemes to gain his favour and to prejudice him against one or another or all but one of his sons-in-law. All of which was not conducive to the peace and repose he had planned for his old age.

He hastened his efforts. For a long time he had been in correspondence with the chief banks in Shanghai and Macao. Every steamer for several years had carried away drafts drawn in favour of one, Chun Ah Chun, for deposit in those Far Eastern banks. The drafts now became heavier. His two youngest daughters were not yet married. He did not wait, but dowered them with a hundred thousand each, which sums lay in the Bank of Hawaii, drawing interest and awaiting their wedding day. Albert took over the business of the firm of Ah Chun and Ah Yung, Harold, the eldest, having elected to take a quarter of a million and go to England to live. Charles, the youngest, took a hundred thousand, a legal guardian, and a course in a Keeley institute. To Mamma Achun was given the bungalow, the mountain House on Tantalus, and a new seaside residence in place of the one Ah Chun sold to the government. Also, to Mamma Achun was given half a million in money well invested.

Ah Chun was now ready to crack the nut of the problem. One fine morning when the family was at breakfast—he had seen to it that all his sons-in-law and their wives were present—he announced that he was returning to his ancestral soil. In a neat little homily he explained that he had made ample provision for his family, and he laid down various maxims that he was sure, he said, would enable them to dwell together in peace and harmony. Also, he gave business advice to his sons-in-law, preached the virtues of temperate living and safe investments, and gave them the benefit of his encyclopedic knowledge of industrial and business conditions in Hawaii. Then he called for his carriage, and, in the company of the weeping Mamma Achun, was driven down to the Pacific Mail steamer, leaving behind him a panic in the bungalow. Captain Higginson clamoured wildly for an injunction. The daughters shed copious tears. One of their husbands, an ex-Federal judge, questioned Ah Chun's sanity, and hastened to the proper authorities to inquire into it. He returned with the information that Ah Chun had appeared before the commission the day before, demanded an examination, and passed with flying colours. There was nothing to be done, so they went down and said good-bye to the little old man, who waved farewell from the promenade deck as the big steamer poked her nose seaward through the coral reef.

But the little old man was not bound for Canton. He knew his own country too well, and the squeeze of the Mandarins, to venture into it with the tidy bulk of wealth that remained to him. He went to Macao. Now Ah Chun had long exercised the power of a king and he was as imperious as a king. When he landed at Macao and went into the office of the biggest European hotel to register, the clerk closed the book on him. Chinese were not permitted. Ah Chun called for the manager and was treated with contumely. He drove away, but in two hours he was back again. He called the clerk and manager in, gave them a month's salary, and discharged them. He had made himself the owner of the hotel; and in the finest suite he settled down during the many months the gorgeous palace in the suburbs was building for him. In the meantime, with the inevitable ability that was his, he increased the earnings of his big hotel from three per cent to thirty.

The troubles Ah Chun had flown began early. There were sons-in-law that made bad investments, others that played ducks and drakes with the Achun dowries. Ah Chun being out of it, they looked at Mamma Ah Chun and her half million, and, looking, engendered not the best of feeling toward one another. Lawyers waxed fat in the striving to ascertain the construction of trust deeds. Suits, cross-suits, and counter-suits cluttered the Hawaiian courts. Nor did the police courts escape. There were angry encounters in which harsh words and harsher blows were struck. There were such things as flower pots being thrown to add emphasis to winged words. And suits for libel arose that dragged their way through the courts and kept Honolulu agog with excitement over the revelations of the witnesses.

In his palace, surrounded by all dear delights of the Orient, Ah Chun smokes his placid pipe and listens to the turmoil overseas. By each mail steamer, in faultless English, typewritten on an American machine, a letter goes from Macao to Honolulu, in which, by admirable texts and precepts, Ah Chun advises his family to live in unity and harmony. As for himself, he is out of it all, and well content. He has won to peace and repose. At times he chuckles and rubs his hands, and his slant little black eyes twinkle merrily at the thought of the funny world. For out of all his living and philosophizing, that remains to him—the conviction that it is a very funny world.

THE SHERIFF OF KONA

"You cannot escape liking the climate," Cudworth said, in reply to my panegyric on the Kona coast. "I was a young fellow, just out of college, when I came here eighteen years ago. I never went back, except, of course, to visit. And I warn you, if you have some spot dear to you on earth, not to linger here too long, else you will find this dearer."

We had finished dinner, which had been served on the big lanai, the one with a northerly exposure, though exposure is indeed a misnomer in so delectable a climate.

The candles had been put out, and a slim, white-clad Japanese slipped like a ghost through the silvery moonlight, presented us with cigars, and faded away into the darkness of the bungalow. I looked through a screen of banana and lehua trees, and down across the guava scrub to the quiet sea a thousand feet beneath. For a week, ever since I had landed from the tiny coasting-steamer, I had been stopping with Cudworth, and during that time no wind had ruffled that unvexed sea. True, there had been breezes, but they were the gentlest zephyrs that ever blew through summer isles. They were not winds; they were sighs—long, balmy sighs of a world at rest.

"A lotus land," I said.

"Where each day is like every day, and every day is a paradise of days," he answered. "Nothing ever happens. It is not too hot. It is not too cold. It is always just right. Have you noticed how the land and the sea breathe turn and turn about?"

Indeed, I had noticed that delicious rhythmic, breathing. Each morning I had watched the sea-breeze begin at the shore and slowly extend seaward as it blew the mildest, softest whiff of ozone to the land. It played over the sea, just faintly darkening its surface, with here and there and everywhere long lanes of calm, shifting, changing, drifting, according to the capricious kisses of the breeze. And each evening I had watched the sea breath die away to heavenly calm, and heard the land breath softly make its way through the coffee trees and monkey-pods.

"It is a land of perpetual calm," I said. "Does it ever blow here?—ever really blow? You know what I mean."

Cudworth shook his head and pointed eastward.

"How can it blow, with a barrier like that to stop it?"

Far above towered the huge bulks of Mauna Kea and Mauna Loa, seeming to blot out half the starry sky. Two miles and a half above our heads they reared their own heads, white with snow that the tropic sun had failed to melt.

"Thirty miles away, right now, I'll wager, it is blowing forty miles an hour."

I smiled incredulously.

Cudworth stepped to the lanai telephone. He called up, in succession, Waimea, Kohala, and Hamakua. Snatches of his conversation told me that the wind was blowing: "Rip-snorting and back-jumping, eh? . . . How long? . . . Only a week? . . . Hello, Abe, is that you? . . . Yes, yes . . . You will plant coffee on the Hamakua coast . . . Hang your wind-breaks! You should see my trees."

"Blowing a gale," he said to me, turning from hanging up the receiver. "I always have to joke Abe on his coffee. He has five hundred acres, and he's done marvels in wind-breaking, but how he keeps the roots in the ground is beyond me. Blow? It always blows on the Hamakua side. Kohala reports a schooner under double reefs beating up the channel between Hawaii and Maui, and making heavy weather of it."

"It is hard to realize," I said lamely. "Doesn't a little whiff of it ever eddy around somehow, and get down here?"

"Not a whiff. Our land-breeze is absolutely of no kin, for it begins this side of Mauna Kea and Mauna Loa. You see, the land radiates its heat quicker than the sea, and so, at night, the land breathes over the sea. In the day the land becomes warmer than the sea, and the sea breathes over the land . . . Listen! Here comes the land-breath now, the mountain wind."

I could hear it coming, rustling softly through the coffee trees, stirring the monkey-pods, and sighing through the sugar-cane. On the lanai the hush still reigned. Then it came, the first feel of the mountain wind, faintly balmy, fragrant and spicy, and cool, deliciously cool, a silken coolness, a wine-like coolness—cool as only the mountain wind of Kona can be cool.

"Do you wonder that I lost my heart to Kona eighteen years ago?" he demanded. "I could never leave it now. I think I should die. It would be terrible. There was another man who loved it, even as I. I think he loved it more, for he was born here on the Kona coast. He was a great man, my best friend, my more than brother. But he left it, and he did not die."

"Love?" I queried. "A woman?"

Cudworth shook his head.

"Nor will he ever come back, though his heart will be here until he dies."

He paused and gazed down upon the beachlights of Kailua. I smoked silently and waited.

"He was already in love . . . with his wife. Also, he had three children, and he loved them. They are in Honolulu now. The boy is going to college."

"Some rash act?" I questioned, after a time, impatiently.

He shook his head. "Neither guilty of anything criminal, nor charged with anything criminal. He was the Sheriff of Kona."

"You choose to be paradoxical," I said.

"I suppose it does sound that way," he admitted, "and that is the perfect hell of it."

He looked at me searchingly for a moment, and then abruptly took up the tale.

"He was a leper. No, he was not born with it—no one is born with it; it came upon him. This man—what does it matter? Lyte Gregory was his name. Every kamaina knows the story. He was straight American stock, but he was built like the chieftains of old Hawaii. He stood six feet three. His stripped weight was two hundred and twenty pounds, not an ounce of which was not clean muscle or bone. He was the strongest man I have ever seen. He was an athlete and a giant. He was a god. He was my friend. And his heart and his soul were as big and as fine as his body.

"I wonder what you would do if you saw your friend, your brother, on the slippery lip of a precipice, slipping, slipping, and you were able to do nothing. That was just it. I could do nothing. I saw it coming, and I could do nothing. My God, man, what could I do? There it was, malignant and incontestable, the mark of the thing on his brow. No one else saw it. It was because I loved him so, I do believe, that I alone saw it. I could not credit the testimony of my senses. It was too incredibly horrible. Yet there it was, on his brow, on his ears. I had seen it, the slight puff of the earlobes—oh, so imperceptibly slight. I watched it for months. Then, next, hoping against hope, the darkening of the skin above both eyebrows—oh, so faint, just like the dimmest touch of sunburn. I should have thought it sunburn but that there was a shine to it, such an invisible shine, like a little highlight seen for a moment and gone the next. I tried to believe it was sunburn, only I could not. I knew better. No one noticed it but me. No one ever noticed it except Stephen Kaluna, and I did not know that till afterward. But I saw it coming, the whole damnable, unnamable awfulness of it; but I refused to think about the future. I was afraid. I could not. And of nights I cried over it.

"He was my friend. We fished sharks on Niihau together. We hunted wild cattle on Mauna Kea and Mauna Loa. We broke horses and branded steers on the Carter Ranch. We hunted goats through Haleakala. He taught me diving and surfing until I was nearly as clever as he, and he was cleverer than the average Kanaka. I have seen him dive in fifteen fathoms, and he could stay down two minutes. He was an amphibian and a mountaineer. He could climb wherever a goat dared climb. He was afraid of nothing. He was on the wrecked Luga, and he swam thirty miles in thirty-six hours in a heavy sea. He could fight his way out through breaking combers that would batter you and me to a jelly. He was a great, glorious man-god. We went through the Revolution together. We were both romantic loyalists. He was shot twice and sentenced to death. But he was too great a man for the republicans to kill. He laughed at them. Later, they gave him honour and made him Sheriff of Kona. He was a simple man, a boy that never grew up. His was no intricate brain pattern. He had no twists nor quirks in his mental processes. He went straight to the point, and his points were always simple.

"And he was sanguine. Never have I known so confident a man, nor a man so satisfied and happy. He did not ask anything from life. There was nothing left to be desired. For him life had no arrears. He had been paid in full, cash down, and in advance. What more could he possibly desire than that magnificent body, that iron constitution, that immunity from all ordinary ills, and that lowly wholesomeness of soul? Physically he was perfect. He had never been sick in his life. He did not know what a headache was. When I was so afflicted he used to look at me in wonder, and make me laugh with his clumsy attempts at sympathy. He did not understand such a thing as a headache. He could not understand. Sanguine? No wonder. How could he be otherwise with that tremendous vitality and incredible health?

"Just to show you what faith he had in his glorious star, and, also, what sanction he had for that faith. He was a youngster at the time—I had just met him—when he went into a poker game at Wailuku. There was a big German in it, Schultz his name was, and he played a brutal, domineering game. He had had a run of luck as well, and he was quite insufferable, when Lyte Gregory dropped in and took a hand. The very first hand it was Schultz's blind. Lyte came in, as well as the others, and Schultz raised them out—all except Lyte. He did not like the German's tone, and he raised him back. Schultz raised in turn, and in turn Lyte raised Schultz. So they went, back and forth. The stakes were big. And do you know what Lyte held? A pair of kings and three little clubs. It wasn't poker. Lyte wasn't playing poker. He was playing his optimism. He didn't know what Schultz held, but he raised and raised until he made Schultz squeal, and Schultz held three aces all the time. Think of it! A man with a pair of kings compelling three aces to see before the draw!

"Well, Schultz called for two cards. Another German was dealing, Schultz's friend at that. Lyte knew then that he was up against three of a kind. Now what did he do? What would you have done? Drawn three cards and held up the kings, of course. Not Lyte. He was playing optimism. He threw the kings away, held up the three little clubs, and drew two cards. He never looked at them. He looked across at Schultz to bet, and Schultz did bet, big. Since he himself held three aces he knew he had Lyte, because he played Lyte for threes, and, necessarily, they would have to be smaller threes. Poor Schultz! He was perfectly correct under the premises. His mistake was that he thought Lyte was playing poker. They bet back and forth for five minutes, until Schultz's certainty began to ooze out. And all the time Lyte had never looked at his two cards, and Schultz knew it. I could see Schultz think, and revive, and splurge with his bets again. But the strain was too much for him."

"'Hold on, Gregory,' he said at last. 'I've got you beaten from the start. I don't want any of your money. I've got—'"

"'Never mind what you've got,' Lyte interrupted. 'You don't know what I've got. I guess I'll take a look.'"

"He looked, and raised the German a hundred dollars. Then they went at it again, back and forth and back and forth, until Schultz weakened and called, and laid down his three aces. Lyte faced his five cards. They were all black. He had drawn two more clubs. Do you know, he just about broke Schultz's nerve as a poker player. He never played in the same form again. He lacked confidence after that, and was a bit wobbly."

"'But how could you do it?' I asked Lyte afterwards. 'You knew he had you beaten when he drew two cards. Besides, you never looked at your own draw.'"

"'I didn't have to look,' was Lyte's answer. 'I knew they were two clubs all the time. They just had to be two clubs. Do you think I was going to let that big Dutchman beat me? It was impossible that he should beat me. It is not my way to be beaten. I just have to win. Why, I'd have been the most surprised man in this world if they hadn't been all clubs.'"

"That was Lyte's way, and maybe it will help you to appreciate his colossal optimism. As he put it he just had to succeed, to fare well, to prosper. And in that same incident, as in ten thousand others, he found his sanction. The thing was that he did succeed, did prosper. That was why he was afraid of nothing. Nothing could ever happen to him. He knew it, because nothing had ever happened to him. That time the Luga was lost and he swam thirty miles, he was in the water two whole nights and a day. And during all that terrible stretch of time he never lost hope once, never once doubted the outcome. He just knew he was going to make the land. He told me so himself, and I know it was the truth.

"Well, that is the kind of a man Lyte Gregory was. He was of a different race from ordinary, ailing mortals. He was a lordly being, untouched by common ills and misfortunes. Whatever he wanted he got. He won his wife—one of the Caruthers, a little beauty—from a dozen rivals. And she settled down and made him the finest wife in the world. He wanted a boy. He got it. He wanted a girl and another boy. He got them. And they were just right, without spot or blemish, with chests like little barrels, and with all the inheritance of his own health and strength.

"And then it happened. The mark of the beast was laid upon him. I watched it for a year. It broke my heart. But he did not know it, nor did anybody else guess it except that cursed hapa-haole, Stephen Kaluna. He knew it, but I did not know that he did. And—yes—Doc Strowbridge knew it. He was the federal physician, and he had developed the leper eye. You see, part of his business was to examine suspects and order them to the receiving station at Honolulu. And Stephen Kaluna had developed the leper eye. The disease ran strong in his family, and four or five of his relatives were already on Molokai.

"The trouble arose over Stephen Kaluna's sister. When she became suspect, and before Doc Strowbridge could get hold of her, her brother spirited her away to some hiding-place. Lyte was Sheriff of Kona, and it was his business to find her.

"We were all over at Hilo that night, in Ned Austin's. Stephen Kaluna was there when we came in, by himself, in his cups, and quarrelsome. Lyte was laughing over some joke—that huge, happy laugh of a giant boy. Kaluna spat contemptuously on the floor. Lyte noticed, so did everybody; but he ignored the fellow. Kaluna was looking for trouble. He took it as a personal grudge that Lyte was trying to apprehend his sister. In half a dozen ways he advertised his displeasure at Lyte's presence, but Lyte ignored him. I imagined Lyte was a bit sorry for him, for the hardest duty of his office was the apprehension of lepers. It is not a nice thing to go in to a man's house and tear away a father, mother, or child, who has done no wrong, and to send such a one to perpetual banishment on Molokai. Of course, it is necessary as a protection to society, and Lyte, I do believe, would have been the first to apprehend his own father did he become suspect.

"Finally, Kaluna blurted out: 'Look here, Gregory, you think you're going to find Kalaniweo, but you're not.'

"Kalaniweo was his sister. Lyte glanced at him when his name was called, but he made no answer. Kaluna was furious. He was working himself up all the time.

"'I'll tell you one thing,' he shouted. 'You'll be on Molokai yourself before ever you get Kalaniweo there. I'll tell you what you are. You've no right to be in the company of honest men. You've made a terrible fuss talking about your duty, haven't you? You've sent many lepers to Molokai, and knowing all the time you belonged there yourself.'

"I'd seen Lyte angry more than once, but never quite so angry as at that moment. Leprosy with us, you know, is not a thing to jest about. He made one leap across the floor, dragging Kaluna out of his chair with a clutch on his neck. He shook him back and forth savagely, till you could hear the half-caste's teeth rattling.

"'What do you mean?' Lyte was demanding. 'Spit it out, man, or I'll choke it out of you!'

"You know, in the West there is a certain phrase that a man must smile while uttering. So with us of the islands, only our phrase is related to leprosy. No matter what Kaluna was, he was no coward. As soon as Lyte eased the grip on his throat he answered:—

"'I'll tell you what I mean. You are a leper yourself.'

"Lyte suddenly flung the half-caste sideways into a chair, letting him down easily enough. Then Lyte broke out into honest, hearty laughter. But he laughed alone, and when he discovered it he looked around at our faces. I had reached his side and was trying to get him to come away, but he took no notice of me. He was gazing, fascinated, at Kaluna, who was brushing at his own throat in a flurried, nervous way, as if to brush off the contamination of the fingers that had clutched him. The action was unreasoned, genuine.

"Lyte looked around at us, slowly passing from face to face.

"'My God, fellows! My God!' he said.

"He did not speak it. It was more a hoarse whisper of fright and horror. It was fear that fluttered in his throat, and I don't think that ever in his life before he had known fear.

"Then his colossal optimism asserted itself, and he laughed again.

"'A good joke—whoever put it up,' he said. 'The drinks are on me. I had a scare for a moment. But, fellows, don't do it again, to anybody. It's too serious. I tell you I died a thousand deaths in that moment. I thought of my wife and the kids, and . . . '

"His voice broke, and the half-caste, still throat-brushing, drew his eyes. He was puzzled and worried.

"'John,' he said, turning toward me.

"His jovial, rotund voice rang in my ears. But I could not answer. I was swallowing hard at that moment, and besides, I knew my face didn't look just right.

"'John,' he called again, taking a step nearer.

"He called timidly, and of all nightmares of horrors the most frightful was to hear timidity in Lyte Gregory's voice.

"'John, John, what does it mean?' he went on, still more timidly. 'It's a joke, isn't it? John, here's my hand. If I were a leper would I offer you my hand? Am I a leper, John?'

"He held out his hand, and what in high heaven or hell did I care? He was my friend. I took his hand, though it cut me to the heart to see the way his face brightened.

"'It was only a joke, Lyte,' I said. 'We fixed it up on you. But you're right. It's too serious. We won't do it again.'

"He did not laugh this time. He smiled, as a man awakened from a bad dream and still oppressed by the substance of the dream.

"'All right, then,' he said. 'Don't do it again, and I'll stand for the drinks. But I may as well confess that you fellows had me going south for a moment. Look at the way I've been sweating.'

"He sighed and wiped the sweat from his forehead as he started to step toward the bar.

"'It is no joke,' Kaluna said abruptly. I looked murder at him, and I felt murder, too. But I dared not speak or strike. That would have precipitated the catastrophe which I somehow had a mad hope of still averting.

"'It is no joke,' Kaluna repeated. 'You are a leper, Lyte Gregory, and you've no right putting your hands on honest men's flesh—on the clean flesh of honest men.'

"Then Gregory flared up.

"'The joke has gone far enough! Quit it! Quit it, I say, Kaluna, or I'll give you a beating!'

"'You undergo a bacteriological examination,' Kaluna answered, 'and then you can beat me—to death, if you want to. Why, man, look at yourself there in the glass. You can see it. Anybody can see it. You're developing the lion face. See where the skin is darkened there over your eyes.

"Lyte peered and peered, and I saw his hands trembling.

"'I can see nothing,' he said finally, then turned on the hapa-haole. 'You have a black heart, Kaluna. And I am not ashamed to say that you have given me a scare that no man has a right to give another. I take you at your word. I am going to settle this thing now. I am going straight to Doc Strowbridge. And when I come back, watch out.'

"He never looked at us, but started for the door.

"'You wait here, John,' he said, waving me back from accompanying him.

"We stood around like a group of ghosts.

"'It is the truth,' Kaluna said. 'You could see it for yourselves.'

"They looked at me, and I nodded. Harry Burnley lifted his glass to his lips, but lowered it untasted. He spilled half of it over the bar. His lips were trembling like a child that is about to cry. Ned Austin made a clatter in the ice-chest. He wasn't looking for anything. I don't think he knew what he was doing. Nobody spoke. Harry Burnley's lips were trembling harder than ever. Suddenly, with a most horrible, malignant expression he drove his fist into Kaluna's face. He followed it up. We made no attempt to separate them. We didn't care if he killed the half-caste. It was a terrible beating. We weren't interested. I don't even remember when Burnley ceased and let the poor devil crawl away. We were all too dazed.

"Doc Strowbridge told me about it afterward. He was working late over a report when Lyte came into his office. Lyte had already recovered his optimism, and came swinging in, a trifle angry with Kaluna to be sure, but very certain of himself. 'What could I do?' Doc asked me. 'I knew he had it. I had seen it coming on for months. I couldn't answer him. I couldn't say yes. I don't mind telling you I broke down and cried. He pleaded for the bacteriological test. 'Snip out a piece, Doc,' he said, over and over. 'Snip out a piece of skin and make the test.'"

"The way Doc Strowbridge cried must have convinced Lyte. The

Claudine was leaving next morning for Honolulu. We caught him when he was going aboard. You see, he was headed for Honolulu to give himself up to the Board of Health. We could do nothing with him. He had sent too many to Molokai to hang back himself. We argued for Japan. But he wouldn't hear of it. 'I've got to take my medicine, fellows,' was all he would say, and he said it over and over. He was obsessed with the idea.

"He wound up all his affairs from the Receiving Station at Honolulu, and went down to Molokai. He didn't get on well there. The resident physician wrote us that he was a shadow of his old self. You see he was grieving about his wife and the kids. He knew we were taking care of them, but it hurt him just the same. After six months or so I went down to Molokai. I sat on one side a plate-glass window, and he on the other. We looked at each other through the glass and talked through what might be called a speaking tube. But it was hopeless. He had made up his mind to remain. Four mortal hours I argued. I was exhausted at the end. My steamer was whistling for me, too.

"But we couldn't stand for it. Three months later we chartered the schooner Halcyon. She was an opium smuggler, and she sailed like a witch. Her master was a squarehead who would do anything for money, and we made a charter to China worth his while. He sailed from San Francisco, and a few days later we took out Landhouse's sloop for a cruise. She was only a five-ton yacht, but we slammed her fifty miles to windward into the northeast trade. Seasick? I never suffered so in my life. Out of sight of land we picked up the Halcyon, and Burnley and I went aboard.

"We ran down to Molokai, arriving about eleven at night. The schooner hove to and we landed through the surf in a whale-boat at Kalawao—the place, you know, where Father Damien died. That squarehead was game. With a couple of revolvers strapped on him he came right along. The three of us crossed the peninsula to Kalaupapa, something like two miles. Just imagine hunting in the dead of night for a man in a settlement of over a thousand lepers. You see, if the alarm was given, it was all off with us. It was strange ground, and pitch dark. The leper's dogs came out and bayed at us, and we stumbled around till we got lost.

"The squarehead solved it. He led the way into the first detached house.

We shut the door after us and struck a light. There were six lepers. We routed them up, and I talked in native. What I wanted was a kokua. A kokua is, literally, a helper, a native who is clean that lives in the settlement and is paid by the Board of Health to nurse the lepers, dress their sores, and such things. We stayed in the house to keep track of the inmates, while the squarehead led one of them off to find a kokua. He got him, and he brought him along at the point of his revolver. But the kokua was all right. While the squarehead guarded the house, Burnley and I were guided by the kokua to Lyte's house. He was all alone.

"'I thought you fellows would come,' Lyte said. 'Don't touch me, John. How's Ned, and Charley, and all the crowd? Never mind, tell me afterward. I am ready to go now. I've had nine months of it. Where's the boat?'

"We started back for the other house to pick up the squarehead. But the alarm had got out. Lights were showing in the houses, and doors were slamming. We had agreed that there was to be no shooting unless absolutely necessary, and when we were halted we went at it with our fists and the butts of our revolvers. I found myself tangled up with a big man. I couldn't keep him off me, though twice I smashed him fairly in the face with my fist. He grappled with me, and we went down, rolling and scrambling and struggling for grips. He was getting away with me, when some one came running up with a lantern. Then I saw his face. How shall I describe the horror of it. It was not a face—only wasted or wasting features—a living ravage, noseless, lipless, with one ear swollen and distorted, hanging down to the shoulder. I was frantic. In a clinch he hugged me close to him until that ear flapped in my face. Then I guess I went insane. It was too terrible. I began striking him with my revolver. How it happened I don't know, but just as I was getting clear he fastened upon me with his teeth. The whole side of my hand was in that lipless mouth. Then I struck him with the revolver butt squarely between the eyes, and his teeth relaxed."

Cudworth held his hand to me in the moonlight, and I could see the scars. It looked as if it had been mangled by a dog.

"Weren't you afraid?" I asked.

"I was. Seven years I waited. You know, it takes that long for the disease to incubate. Here in Kona I waited, and it did not come. But there was never a day of those seven years, and never a night, that I did not look out on . . . on all this . . . " His voice broke as he swept his eyes from the moon-bathed sea beneath to the snowy summits above. "I could not bear to think of losing it, of never again beholding Kona. Seven years! I stayed clean. But that is why I am single. I was engaged. I could not dare to marry while I was in doubt. She did not understand. She went away to the States and married. I have never seen her since.

"Just at the moment I got clear of the leper policeman there was a rush and clatter of hoofs like a cavalry charge. It was the squarehead. He had been afraid of a rumpus and he had improved his time by making those blessed lepers he was guarding saddle up four horses. We were ready for him. Lyte had accounted for three kokuas, and between us we untangled Burnley from a couple more. The whole settlement was in an uproar by that time, and as we dashed away somebody opened upon us with a Winchester. It must have been Jack McVeigh, the superintendent of Molokai.

"That was a ride! Leper horses, leper saddles, leper bridles, pitch-black darkness, whistling bullets, and a road none of the best. And the squarehead's horse was a mule, and he didn't know how to ride, either. But we made the whaleboat, and as we shoved off through the surf we could hear the horses coming down the hill from Kalaupapa.

"You're going to Shanghai. You look Lyte Gregory up. He is employed in a German firm there. Take him out to dinner. Open up wine. Give him everything of the best, but don't let him pay for anything. Send the bill to me. His wife and the kids are in Honolulu, and he needs the money for them. I know. He sends most of his salary, and lives like an anchorite. And tell him about Kona. There's where his heart is. Tell him all you can about Kona."

JACK LONDON BY HIMSELF

I was born in San Francisco in 1876. At fifteen I was a man among men, and if I had a spare nickel I spent it on beer instead of candy, because I thought it was more manly to buy beer. Now, when my years are nearly doubled, I am out on a hunt for the boyhood which I never had, and I am less serious than at any other time of my life. Guess I'll find that boyhood! Almost the first things I realized were responsibilities. I have no recollection of being taught to read or write—I could do both at the age of five—but I know that my first school was in Alameda before I went out on a ranch with my folks and as a ranch boy worked hard from my eighth year.

The second school were I tried to pick up a little learning was an irregular hit or miss affair at San Mateo. Each class sat in a separate desk, but there were days when we did not sit at all, for the master used to get drunk very often, and then one of the elder boys would thrash him. To even things up, the master would then thrash the younger lads, so you can think what sort of school it was. There was no one belonging to me, or associated with me in any way, who had literary tastes or ideas, the nearest I can make to it is that my great-grandfather was a circuit writer, a Welshman, known as "Priest" Jones in the backwoods, where his enthusiasm led him to scatter the Gospel.

One of my earliest and strongest impressions was of the ignorance of other people. I had read and absorbed Washington Irving's "Alhambra" before I was nine, but could never understand how it was that the other ranchers knew nothing about it. Later I concluded that this ignorance was peculiar to the country, and felt that those who lived in cities would not be so dense. One day a man from the city came to the ranch. He wore shiny shoes and a cloth coat, and I felt that here was a good chance for me to exchange thoughts with an enlightened mind. From the bricks of an old fallen chimney I had built an Alhambra of my own; towers, terraces, and all were complete, and chalk inscriptions marked the different sections. Here I led the city man and questioned him about "The Alhambra," but he was as ignorant as the man on the ranch, and then I consoled myself with the thought that there were only two clever people in the world—Washington Irving and myself.

My other reading-matter at that time consisted mainly of dime novels, borrowed from the hired men, and newspapers in which the servants gloated over the adventures of poor but virtuous shop-girls.

Through reading such stuff my mind was necessarily ridiculously conventional, but being very lonely I read everything that came my way, and was greatly impressed by Ouida's story "Signa," which I devoured regularly for a couple of years. I never knew the finish until I grew up, for the closing chapters were missing from my copy, so I kept on dreaming with the hero, and, like him, unable to see Nemesis, at the end. My work on the ranch at one time was to watch the bees, and as I sat under a tree from sunrise till late in the afternoon, waiting for the swarming, I had plenty of time to read and dream. Livermore Valley was very flat, and even the hills around were then to me devoid of interest, and the only incident to break in on my visions was when I gave the alarm of swarming, and the ranch folks rushed out with pots, pans, and buckets of water. I think the opening line of "Signa" was "It was only a little lad," yet he had dreams of becoming a great musician, and having all Europe at his feet. Well, I was only a little lad, too, but why could not I become what "Signa" dreamed of being?

Life on a Californian ranch was then to me the dullest possible existence, and every day I thought of going out beyond the sky-line to see the world. Even then there were whispers, promptings; my mind inclined to things beautiful, although my environment was unbeautiful. The hills and valleys around were eyesores and aching pits, and I never loved them till I left them.

* * * * *

Before I was eleven I left the ranch and came to Oakland, where I spent so much of my time in the Free Public Library, eagerly reading everything that came to hand, that I developed the first stages of St. Vitus' dance from lack of exercise. Disillusions quickly followed, as I learned more of the world. At this time I made my living as a newsboy, selling papers in the streets; and from then on until I was sixteen I had a thousand and one different occupations—work and school, school and work—and so it ran.

Then the adventure-lust was strong within me, and I left home. I didn't run, I just left—went out in the bay, and joined the oyster pirates. The days of the oyster pirates are now past, and if I had got my dues for piracy, I would have been given five hundred years in prison. Later, I shipped as a sailor on a schooner, and also took a turn at salmon fishing. Oddly enough, my next occupation was on a fish-patrol, where I was entrusted with the arrest of any violators of the fishing laws. Numbers of lawless Chinese, Greeks, and Italians were at that time engaged in illegal fishing, and many a patrolman paid his life for his interference. My only weapon on duty was a steel table-fork, but I felt fearless and a man when I climbed over the side of a boat to arrest some marauder.

Subsequently I shipped before the mast and sailed for the Japanese coast on a seal-hunting expedition, later going to Behring Sea. After sealing for seven months I came back to California and took odd jobs at coal shovelling and longshoring and also in a jute factory, where I worked from six in the morning until seven at night. I had planned to join the same lot for another sealing trip the following year, but somehow I missed them. They sailed away on the Mary Thomas, which was lost with all hands.

In my fitful school-days I had written the usual compositions, which had been praised in the usual way, and while working in the jute mills I still made an occasional try. The factory occupied thirteen hours of my day, and being young and husky, I wanted a little time for myself, so there was little left for composition. The San Francisco Call offered a prize for a descriptive article. My mother urged me to try for it, and I did, taking for my subject "Typhoon off the Coast of Japan." Very tired and sleepy, knowing I had to be up at half-past five, I began the article at midnight and worked straight on until I had written two thousand words, the limit of the article, but with my idea only half worked out. The next night, under the same conditions, I continued, adding another two thousand words before I finished, and then the third night I spent in cutting out the excess, so as to bring the article within the conditions of the contest. The first prize came to me, and the second and third went to students of the Stanford and Berkeley Universities.

My success in the San Francisco Call competition seriously turned my thoughts to writing, but my blood was still too hot for a settled routine, so I practically deferred literature, beyond writing a little gush for the Call, which that journal promptly rejected.

I tramped all through the United States, from California to Boston, and up and down, returning to the Pacific coast by way of Canada, where I got into jail and served a term for vagrancy, and the whole tramping experience made me become a Socialist. Previously I had been impressed by the dignity of labour, and, without having read Carlyle or Kipling, I had formulated a gospel of work which put theirs in the shade. Work was everything. It was sanctification and salvation. The pride I took in a hard day's work well done would be inconceivable to you. I was as faithful a wage-slave as ever a capitalist exploited. In short, my joyous individualism was dominated by the orthodox bourgeois ethics. I had fought my way from the open west, where men bucked big and the job hunted the man, to the congested labour centres of the eastern states, where men were small potatoes and hunted the job for all they were worth, and I found myself looking upon life from a new and totally different angle. I saw the workers in the shambles at the bottom of the Social Pit. I swore I would never again do a hard day's work with my body except where absolutely compelled to, and I have been busy ever since running away from hard bodily labour.

In my nineteenth year I returned to Oakland and started at the High School, which ran the usual school magazine. This publication was a weekly— no, I guess a monthly—one, and I wrote stories for it, very little imaginary, just recitals of my sea and tramping experiences. I remained there a year, doing janitor work as a means of livelihood, and leaving eventually because the strain was more than I could bear. At this time my socialistic utterances had attracted considerable attention, and I was known as the "Boy Socialist," a distinction that brought about my arrest for street-talking. After leaving the High School, in three months cramming by myself, I took the three years' work for that time and entered the University of California. I hated to give up the hope of a University education and worked in a laundry and with my pen to help me keep on. This was the only time I worked because I loved it, but the task was too much, and when half-way through my Freshman year I had to quit.

I worked away ironing shirts and other things in the laundry, and wrote in all my spare time. I tried to keep on at both, but often fell asleep with the pen in my hand. Then I left the laundry and wrote all the time, and lived and dreamed again. After three months' trial I gave up writing, having decided that I was a failure, and left for the Klondike to prospect for gold. At the end of the year, owing to the outbreak of scurvy, I was compelled to come out, and on the homeward journey of 1,900 miles in an open boat made the only notes of the trip. It was in the Klondike I found myself. There nobody talks. Everybody thinks. You get your true perspective. I got mine.

While I was in the Klondike my father died, and the burden of the family fell on my shoulders. Times were bad in California, and I could get no work. While trying for it I wrote "Down the River," which was rejected. During the wait for this rejection I wrote a twenty-thousand word serial for a news company, which was also rejected. Pending each rejection I still kept on writing fresh stuff. I did not know what an editor looked like. I did not know a soul who had ever published anything. Finally a story was accepted by a Californian magazine, for which I received five dollars. Soon afterwards "The Black Cat" offered me forty dollars for a story.

Then things took a turn, and I shall probably not have to shovel coal for a living for some time to come, although I have done it, and could do it again.

My first book was published in 1900. I could have made a good deal at newspaper work; but I had sufficient sense to refuse to be a slave to that man-killing machine, for such I held a newspaper to be to a young man in his forming period. Not until I was well on my feet as a magazine-writer did I do much work for newspapers. I am a believer in regular work, and never wait for an inspiration. Temperamentally I am not only careless and irregular, but melancholy; still I have fought both down. The discipline I had as a sailor had full effect on me. Perhaps my old sea days are also responsible for the regularity and limitations of my sleep. Five and a half hours is the precise average I allow myself, and no circumstance has yet arisen in my life that could keep me awake when the time comes to "turn in."

I am very fond of sport, and delight in boxing, fencing, swimming, riding, yachting, and even kite-flying. Although primarily of the city, I like to be near it rather than in it. The country, though, is the best, the only natural life. In my grown-up years the writers who have influenced me most are Karl Marx in a particular, and Spencer in a general, way. In the days of my barren boyhood, if I had had a chance, I would have gone in for music; now, in what are more genuinely the days of my youth, if I had a million or two I would devote myself to writing poetry and pamphlets. I think the best work I have done is in the "League of the Old Men," and parts of "The Kempton-Wace Letters." Other people don't like the former. They prefer brighter and more cheerful things. Perhaps I shall feel like that, too, when the days of my youth are behind me.

Footnotes:

[1] Malahini—new-comer.

About Author

Family

Jack London's mother, Flora Wellman, was the fifth and youngest child of Pennsylvania Canal builder Marshall Wellman and his first wife, Eleanor Garrett Jones. Marshall Wellman was descended from Thomas Wellman, an early Puritan settler in the Massachusetts Bay Colony. Flora left Ohio and moved to the Pacific coast when her father remarried after her mother died. In San Francisco, Flora worked as a music teacher and spiritualist, claiming to channel the spirit of a Sauk chief, Black Hawk.

Biographer Clarice Stasz and others believe London's father was astrologer William Chaney. Flora Wellman was living with Chaney in San Francisco when she became pregnant. Whether Wellman and Chaney were legally married is unknown. Most San Francisco civil records were destroyed by the extensive fires that followed the 1906 earthquake; nobody knows what name appeared on her son's birth certificate. Stasz notes that in his memoirs, Chaney refers to London's mother Flora Wellman as having been his "wife"; he also cites an advertisement in which Flora called herself "Florence Wellman Chaney".

According to Flora Wellman's account, as recorded in the San Francisco Chronicle of June 4, 1875, Chaney demanded that she have an abortion. When she refused, he disclaimed responsibility for the child. In desperation, she shot herself. She was not seriously wounded, but she was temporarily deranged. After giving birth, Flora turned the baby over for care to Virginia Prentiss, an African-American woman and former slave. She was a major maternal figure throughout London's life. Late in 1876, Flora Wellman married John London, a partially disabled Civil War veteran, and brought her baby John, later known as Jack, to live with the newly married couple. The family moved around the San Francisco Bay Area before settling in Oakland, where London completed public grade school.

In 1897, when he was 21 and a student at the University of California, Berkeley, London searched for and read the newspaper accounts of his mother's suicide attempt and the name of his biological father. He wrote to William Chaney, then living in Chicago. Chaney responded that he could not be London's father because he was impotent; he casually asserted that London's mother had relations with other men and averred that she had slandered him when she said he insisted on an abortion. Chaney concluded by saying that he was more to be pitied than London. London was devastated by his father's letter; in the months following, he quit school at Berkeley and went to the Klondike during the gold rush boom.

Early life

London was born near Third and Brannan Streets in San Francisco. The house burned down in the fire after the 1906 San Francisco earthquake; the California Historical Society placed a plaque at the site in 1953. Although the family was working class, it was not as impoverished as London's later accounts claimed. London was largely self-educated.

In 1885, London found and read Ouida's long Victorian novel Signa. He credited this as the seed of his literary success. In 1886, he went to the Oakland Public Library and found a sympathetic librarian, Ina Coolbrith, who encouraged his learning. (She later became California's first poet laureate and an important figure in the San Francisco literary community).

In 1889, London began working 12 to 18 hours a day at Hickmott's Cannery. Seeking a way out, he borrowed money from his foster mother Virginia Prentiss, bought the sloop Razzle-Dazzle from an oyster pirate named French Frank, and became an oyster pirate himself. In his memoir, John Barleycorn, he claims also to have stolen French Frank's mistress Mamie. After a few months, his sloop became damaged beyond repair. London hired on as a member of the California Fish Patrol.

In 1893, he signed on to the sealing schooner Sophie Sutherland, bound for the coast of Japan. When he returned, the country was in the grip of the panic of '93 and Oakland was swept by labor unrest. After grueling jobs in a jute mill and a street-railway power plant, London joined Coxey's Army and began his career as a tramp. In 1894, he spent 30 days for vagrancy in the Erie County Penitentiary at Buffalo, New York. In The Road, he wrote:

Man-handling was merely one of the very minor unprintable horrors of the Erie County Pen. I say 'unprintable'; and in justice I must also say undescribable. They were unthinkable to me until I saw them, and I was no spring chicken in the ways of the world and the awful abysses of human degradation. It would take a deep plummet to reach bottom in the Erie County Pen, and I do but skim lightly and facetiously the surface of things as I there saw them.

After many experiences as a hobo and a sailor, he returned to Oakland and attended Oakland High School. He contributed a number of articles to the high school's magazine, The Aegis. His first published work was "Typhoon off the Coast of Japan", an account of his sailing experiences.

As a schoolboy, London often studied at Heinold's First and Last Chance Saloon, a port-side bar in Oakland. At 17, he confessed to the bar's owner, John Heinold, his desire to attend university and pursue a career as a writer. Heinold lent London tuition money to attend college.

London desperately wanted to attend the University of California, Berkeley. In 1896, after a summer of intense studying to pass certification exams, he was admitted. Financial circumstances forced him to leave in 1897 and he never graduated. No evidence suggests that London wrote for student publications while studying at Berkeley.

While at Berkeley, London continued to study and spend time at Heinold's saloon, where he was introduced to the sailors and adventurers who would influence his writing. In his autobiographical novel, John Barleycorn, London mentioned the pub's likeness seventeen times. Heinold's was the place where London met Alexander McLean, a captain known for his cruelty at sea. London based his protagonist Wolf Larsen, in the novel The Sea-Wolf, on McLean.

Heinold's First and Last Chance Saloon is now unofficially named Jack

London's Rendezvous in his honor.

Gold rush and first success

On July 12, 1897, London (age 21) and his sister's husband Captain Shepard sailed to join the Klondike Gold Rush. This was the setting for some of his first successful stories. London's time in the harsh Klondike, however, was detrimental to his health. Like so many other men who were malnourished in the goldfields, London developed scurvy. His gums became swollen, leading to the loss of his four front teeth. A constant gnawing pain affected his hip and leg muscles, and his face was stricken with marks that always reminded him of the struggles he faced in the Klondike. Father William Judge, "The Saint of Dawson", had a facility in Dawson that provided shelter, food and any available medicine to London and others. His struggles there inspired London's short story, "To Build a Fire" (1902, revised in 1908), which many critics assess as his best.

His landlords in Dawson were mining engineers Marshall Latham Bond and Louis Whitford Bond, educated at Yale and Stanford, respectively. The brothers' father, Judge Hiram Bond, was a wealthy mining investor. The Bonds, especially Hiram, were active Republicans. Marshall Bond's diary mentions friendly sparring with London on political issues as a camp pastime.

London left Oakland with a social conscience and socialist leanings; he returned to become an activist for socialism. He concluded that his only hope of escaping the work "trap" was to get an education and "sell his brains". He saw his writing as a business, his ticket out of poverty, and, he hoped, a means of beating the wealthy at their own game. On returning to California in 1898, London began working to get published, a struggle described in his novel, Martin Eden (serialized in 1908, published in 1909). His first published story since high school was "To the Man On Trail", which has frequently been collected in anthologies. When The Overland Monthly offered him only five dollars for it—and was slow paying—London came close to abandoning his writing career. In his words, "literally and literarily I was saved" when The Black Cat accepted his story "A Thousand Deaths", and paid him $40—the "first money I ever received for a story".

London began his writing career just as new printing technologies enabled lower-cost production of magazines. This resulted in a boom in popular magazines aimed at a wide public audience and a strong market for short fiction. In 1900, he made $2,500 in writing, about $75,000 in today's currency. Among the works he sold to magazines was a short story known as either "Diable" (1902) or "Bâtard" (1904), two editions of the same basic story; London received $141.25 for this story on May 27, 1902. In the text, a cruel French Canadian brutalizes his dog, and the dog retaliates and kills the man. London told some of his critics that man's actions are the main cause of the behavior of their animals, and he would show this in another story, The Call of the Wild.

In early 1903, London sold The Call of the Wild to The Saturday Evening Post for $750, and the book rights to Macmillan for $2,000. Macmillan's promotional campaign propelled it to swift success.

While living at his rented villa on Lake Merritt in Oakland, California, London met poet George Sterling; in time they became best friends. In 1902, Sterling helped London find a home closer to his own in nearby Piedmont. In his letters London addressed Sterling as "Greek", owing to Sterling's aquiline nose and classical profile, and he signed them as "Wolf". London was later to depict Sterling as Russ Brissenden in his autobiographical novel Martin Eden (1910) and as Mark Hall in The Valley of the Moon (1913).

In later life London indulged his wide-ranging interests by accumulating a personal library of 15,000 volumes. He referred to his books as "the tools of my trade".

First marriage (1900–04)

London married Elizabeth "Bessie" Maddern on April 7, 1900, the same day The Son of the Wolf was published. Bess had been part of his circle of friends for a number of years. She was related to stage actresses Minnie Maddern Fiske and Emily Stevens. Stasz says, "Both acknowledged publicly that they were not marrying out of love, but from friendship and a belief that they would produce sturdy children." Kingman says, "they were comfortable together... Jack had made it clear to Bessie that he did not love her, but that he liked her enough to make a successful marriage."

London met Bessie through his friend at Oakland High School, Fred Jacobs; she was Fred's fiancee. Bessie, who tutored at Anderson's University Academy in Alameda California, tutored Jack in preparation for his entrance exams for the University of California at Berkeley in 1896. Jacobs was killed aboard the USAT Scandia in 1897, but Jack and Bessie continued their friendship, which included taking photos and developing the film together. This was the beginning of Jack's passion for photography.

During the marriage, London continued his friendship with Anna Strunsky, co-authoring The Kempton-Wace Letters, an epistolary novel contrasting two philosophies of love. Anna, writing "Dane Kempton's" letters, arguing for a romantic view of marriage, while London, writing "Herbert Wace's" letters, argued for a scientific view, based on Darwinism and eugenics. In the novel, his fictional character contrasted two women he had known.

London's pet name for Bess was "Mother-Girl" and Bess's for London was "Daddy-Boy". Their first child, Joan, was born on January 15, 1901, and their second, Bessie (later called Becky), on October 20, 1902. Both children were born in Piedmont, California. Here London wrote one of his most celebrated works, The Call of the Wild.

While London had pride in his children, the marriage was strained. Kingman says that by 1903 the couple were close to separation as they were "extremely incompatible". "Jack was still so kind and gentle with Bessie that when Cloudsley Johns was a house guest in February 1903 he didn't suspect a breakup of their marriage."

London reportedly complained to friends Joseph Noel and George Sterling:

[Bessie] is devoted to purity. When I tell her morality is only evidence of low blood pressure, she hates me. She'd sell me and the children out for her damned purity. It's terrible. Every time I come back after being away from home for a night she won't let me be in the same room with her if she can help it.

Stasz writes that these were "code words for [Bess's] fear that [Jack] was consorting with prostitutes and might bring home venereal disease."

On July 24, 1903, London told Bessie he was leaving and moved out. During 1904, London and Bess negotiated the terms of a divorce, and the decree was granted on November 11, 1904.

War correspondent (1904)

London accepted an assignment of the San Francisco Examiner to cover the Russo-Japanese War in early 1904, arriving in Yokohama on January 25, 1904. He was arrested by Japanese authorities in Shimonoseki, but released through the intervention of American ambassador Lloyd Griscom. After travelling to Korea, he was again arrested by Japanese authorities for straying too close to the border with Manchuria without official permission, and was sent back to Seoul. Released again, London was permitted to travel with the Imperial Japanese Army to the border, and to observe the Battle of the Yalu.

London asked William Randolph Hearst, the owner of the San Francisco Examiner, to be allowed to transfer to the Imperial Russian Army, where he felt that restrictions on his reporting and his movements would be less severe. However, before this could be arranged, he was arrested for a third time in four months, this time for assaulting his Japanese assistants, whom he accused of stealing the fodder for his horse. Released through the personal intervention of President Theodore Roosevelt, London departed the front in June 1904.

Bohemian Club

On August 18, 1904, London went with his close friend, the poet George Sterling, to "Summer High Jinks" at the Bohemian Grove. London was elected to honorary membership in the Bohemian Club and took part in many activities. Other noted members of the Bohemian Club during this time included Ambrose Bierce, Gelett Burgess, Allan Dunn, John Muir,

Frank Norris, and Herman George Scheffauer.

Beginning in December 1914, London worked on The Acorn Planter, A California Forest Play, to be performed as one of the annual Grove Plays, but it was never selected. It was described as too difficult to set to music. London published The Acorn Planter in 1916.

Second marriage

After divorcing Maddern, London married Charmian Kittredge in 1905. London was introduced to Kittredge in 1900 by her aunt Netta Eames, who was an editor at Overland Monthly magazine in San Francisco. The two met prior to his first marriage but became lovers years later after Jack and Bessie London visited Wake Robin, Netta Eames' Sonoma County resort, in 1903. London was injured when he fell from a buggy, and Netta arranged for Charmian to care for him. The two developed a friendship, as Charmian, Netta, her husband Roscoe, and London were politically aligned with socialist causes. At some point the relationship became romantic, and Jack divorced his wife to marry Charmian, who was five years his senior.

Biographer Russ Kingman called Charmian "Jack's soul-mate, always at his side, and a perfect match." Their time together included numerous trips, including a 1907 cruise on the yacht Snark to Hawaii and Australia. Many of London's stories are based on his visits to Hawaii, the last one for 10 months beginning in December 1915.

The couple also visited Goldfield, Nevada, in 1907, where they were guests of the Bond brothers, London's Dawson City landlords. The Bond brothers were working in Nevada as mining engineers.

London had contrasted the concepts of the "Mother Girl" and the "Mate Woman" in The Kempton-Wace Letters. His pet name for Bess had been "Mother-Girl;" his pet name for Charmian was "Mate-Woman." Charmian's aunt and foster mother, a disciple of Victoria Woodhull, had raised her without prudishness. Every biographer alludes to Charmian's uninhibited sexuality.

Joseph Noel calls the events from 1903 to 1905 "a domestic drama that would have intrigued the pen of an Ibsen.... London's had comedy relief in it and a sort of easy-going romance." In broad outline, London was restless in his first marriage, sought extramarital sexual affairs, and found, in Charmian Kittredge, not only a sexually active and adventurous partner, but his future life-companion. They attempted to have children; one child died at birth, and another pregnancy ended in a miscarriage.

In 1906, London published in Collier's magazine his eye-witness report of the San Francisco earthquake.

Beauty Ranch (1905–16)

In 1905, London purchased a 1,000 acres (4.0 km2) ranch in Glen Ellen, Sonoma County, California, on the eastern slope of Sonoma Mountain, for $26,450. He wrote: "Next to my wife, the ranch is the dearest thing in the world to me." He desperately wanted the ranch to become a successful business enterprise. Writing, always a commercial enterprise with London, now became even more a means to an end: "I write for no other purpose than to add to the beauty that now belongs to me. I write a book for no other reason than to add three or four hundred acres to my magnificent estate."

Stasz writes that London "had taken fully to heart the vision, expressed in his agrarian fiction, of the land as the closest earthly version of Eden ... he educated himself through the study of agricultural manuals and scientific tomes. He conceived of a system of ranching that today would be praised for its ecological wisdom." He was proud to own the first concrete silo in California, a circular piggery that he designed. He hoped to adapt the wisdom of Asian sustainable agriculture to the United States. He hired both Italian and Chinese stonemasons, whose distinctly different styles are obvious.

The ranch was an economic failure. Sympathetic observers such as Stasz treat his projects as potentially feasible, and ascribe their failure to bad luck or to being ahead of their time. Unsympathetic historians such as Kevin Starr suggest that he was a bad manager, distracted by other concerns and impaired by his alcoholism. Starr notes that London was absent from his ranch about

101

six months a year between 1910 and 1916 and says, "He liked the show of managerial power, but not grinding attention to detail .... London's workers laughed at his efforts to play big-time rancher [and considered] the operation a rich man's hobby."

London spent $80,000 ($2,230,000 in current value) to build a 15,000-square-foot (1,400 m2) stone mansion called Wolf House on the property. Just as the mansion was nearing completion, two weeks before the Londons planned to move in, it was destroyed by fire.

London's last visit to Hawaii, beginning in December 1915, lasted eight months. He met with Duke Kahanamoku, Prince Jonah Kūhiō Kalaniana'ole, Queen Lili'uokalani and many others, before returning to his ranch in July 1916. He was suffering from kidney failure, but he continued to work.

The ranch (abutting stone remnants of Wolf House) is now a National Historic Landmark and is protected in Jack London State Historic Park.

Animal activism

London witnessed animal cruelty in the training of circus animals, and his subsequent novels Jerry of the Islands and Michael, Brother of Jerry included a foreword entreating the public to become more informed about this practice. In 1918, the Massachusetts Society for the Prevention of Cruelty to Animals and the American Humane Education Society teamed up to create the Jack London Club, which sought to inform the public about cruelty to circus animals and encourage them to protest this establishment. Support from Club members led to a temporary cessation of trained animal acts at Ringling-Barnum and Bailey in 1925.

Death

London died November 22, 1916, in a sleeping porch in a cottage on his ranch. London had been a robust man but had suffered several serious illnesses, including scurvy in the Klondike. Additionally, during travels on the Snark, he and Charmian picked up unspecified tropical infections, and diseases, including yaws. At the time of his death, he suffered from dysentery,

102

late-stage alcoholism, and uremia; he was in extreme pain and taking morphine.

London's ashes were buried on his property not far from the Wolf House. London's funeral took place on November 26, 1916, attended only by close friends, relatives, and workers of the property. In accordance with his wishes, he was cremated and buried next to some pioneer children, under a rock that belonged to the Wolf House. After Charmian's death in 1955, she was also cremated and then buried with her husband in the same simple spot that her husband chose. The grave is marked by a mossy boulder. The buildings and property were later preserved as Jack London State Historic Park, in Glen Ellen, California.

Suicide debate

Because he was using morphine, many older sources describe London's death as a suicide, and some still do. This conjecture appears to be a rumor, or speculation based on incidents in his fiction writings. His death certificate gives the cause as uremia, following acute renal colic.

The biographer Stasz writes, "Following London's death, for a number of reasons, a biographical myth developed in which he has been portrayed as an alcoholic womanizer who committed suicide. Recent scholarship based upon firsthand documents challenges this caricature." Most biographers, including Russ Kingman, now agree he died of uremia aggravated by an accidental morphine overdose.

London's fiction featured several suicides. In his autobiographical memoir John Barleycorn, he claims, as a youth, to have drunkenly stumbled overboard into the San Francisco Bay, "some maundering fancy of going out with the tide suddenly obsessed me". He said he drifted and nearly succeeded in drowning before sobering up and being rescued by fishermen. In the dénouement of The Little Lady of the Big House, the heroine, confronted by the pain of a mortal gunshot wound, undergoes a physician-assisted suicide by morphine. Also, in Martin Eden, the principal protagonist, who shares certain characteristics with London, drowns himself.

Accusations of plagiarism

London was vulnerable to accusations of plagiarism, both because he was such a conspicuous, prolific, and successful writer and because of his methods of working. He wrote in a letter to Elwyn Hoffman, "expression, you see—with me—is far easier than invention." He purchased plots and novels from the young Sinclair Lewis and used incidents from newspaper clippings as writing material.

In July 1901, two pieces of fiction appeared within the same month: London's "Moon-Face", in the San Francisco Argonaut, and Frank Norris' "The Passing of Cock-eye Blacklock", in Century Magazine. Newspapers showed the similarities between the stories, which London said were "quite different in manner of treatment, [but] patently the same in foundation and motive." London explained both writers based their stories on the same newspaper account. A year later, it was discovered that Charles Forrest McLean had published a fictional story also based on the same incident.

Egerton Ryerson Young claimed The Call of the Wild (1903) was taken from Young's book My Dogs in the Northland (1902). London acknowledged using it as a source and claimed to have written a letter to Young thanking him.

In 1906, the New York World published "deadly parallel" columns showing eighteen passages from London's short story "Love of Life" side by side with similar passages from a nonfiction article by Augustus Biddle and J. K. Macdonald, titled "Lost in the Land of the Midnight Sun". London noted the World did not accuse him of "plagiarism", but only of "identity of time and situation", to which he defiantly "pled guilty".

The most serious charge of plagiarism was based on London's "The Bishop's Vision", Chapter 7 of his novel The Iron Heel (1908). The chapter is nearly identical to an ironic essay that Frank Harris published in 1901, titled "The Bishop of London and Public Morality". Harris was incensed and suggested he should receive 1/60th of the royalties from The Iron Heel, the disputed material constituting about that fraction of the whole novel.

London insisted he had clipped a reprint of the article, which had appeared in an American newspaper, and believed it to be a genuine speech delivered by the Bishop of London.

Views

Atheism

London was an atheist. He is quoted as saying, "I believe that when I am dead, I am dead. I believe that with my death I am just as much obliterated as the last mosquito you and I squashed."

Socialism

London wrote from a socialist viewpoint, which is evident in his novel The Iron Heel. Neither a theorist nor an intellectual socialist, London's socialism grew out of his life experience. As London explained in his essay, "How I Became a Socialist", his views were influenced by his experience with people at the bottom of the social pit. His optimism and individualism faded, and he vowed never to do more hard physical work than necessary. He wrote that his individualism was hammered out of him, and he was politically reborn. He often closed his letters "Yours for the Revolution."

London joined the Socialist Labor Party in April 1896. In the same year, the San Francisco Chronicle published a story about the twenty-year-old London's giving nightly speeches in Oakland's City Hall Park, an activity he was arrested for a year later. In 1901, he left the Socialist Labor Party and joined the new Socialist Party of America. He ran unsuccessfully as the high-profile Socialist candidate for mayor of Oakland in 1901 (receiving 245 votes) and 1905 (improving to 981 votes), toured the country lecturing on socialism in 1906, and published two collections of essays about socialism: The War of the Classes (1905) and Revolution, and other Essays (1906).

Stasz notes that "London regarded the Wobblies as a welcome addition to the Socialist cause, although he never joined them in going so far as to recommend sabotage." Stasz mentions a personal meeting between London and Big Bill Haywood in 1912.

In his late (1913) book The Cruise of the Snark, London writes about appeals to him for membership of the Snark's crew from office workers and other "toilers" who longed for escape from the cities, and of being cheated by workmen.

In his Glen Ellen ranch years, London felt some ambivalence toward socialism and complained about the "inefficient Italian labourers" in his employ. In 1916, he resigned from the Glen Ellen chapter of the Socialist Party, but stated emphatically he did so "because of its lack of fire and fight, and its loss of emphasis on the class struggle." In an unflattering portrait of London's ranch days, California cultural historian Kevin Starr refers to this period as "post-socialist" and says "... by 1911 ... London was more bored by the class struggle than he cared to admit."

Racial views

London shared common concerns among European Americans in California about Asian immigration, described as "the yellow peril"; he used the latter term as the title of a 1904 essay. This theme was also the subject of a story he wrote in 1910 called "The Unparalleled Invasion". Presented as an historical essay set in the future, the story narrates events between 1976 and 1987, in which China, with an ever-increasing population, is taking over and colonizing its neighbors with the intention of taking over the entire Earth. The western nations respond with biological warfare and bombard China with dozens of the most infectious diseases. On his fears about China, he admits, "it must be taken into consideration that the above postulate is itself a product of Western race-egotism, urged by our belief in our own righteousness and fostered by a faith in ourselves which may be as erroneous as are most fond race fancies."

By contrast, many of London's short stories are notable for their empathetic portrayal of Mexican ("The Mexican"), Asian ("The Chinago"), and Hawaiian ("Koolau the Leper") characters. London's war correspondence from the Russo-Japanese War, as well as his unfinished novel Cherry, show he admired much about Japanese customs and capabilities. London's writings have been popular among the Japanese, who believe he portrayed them positively.

In "Koolau the Leper", London describes Koolau, who is a Hawaiian leper—and thus a very different sort of "superman" than Martin Eden—and who fights off an entire cavalry troop to elude capture, as "indomitable spiritually—a ... magnificent rebel". This character is based on Hawaiian leper Kaluaikoolau, who in 1893 revolted and resisted capture from forces of the Provisional Government of Hawaii in the Kalalau Valley.

An amateur boxer and avid boxing fan, London reported on the 1910 Johnson–Jeffries fight, in which the black boxer Jack Johnson vanquished Jim Jeffries, known as the "Great White Hope". In 1908, London had reported on an earlier fight of Johnson's, contrasting the black boxer's coolness and intellectual style, with the apelike appearance and fighting style of his Canadian opponent, Tommy Burns,

'what . . . [won] on Saturday was bigness, coolness, quickness, cleverness, and vast physical superiority... Because a white man wishes a white man to win, this should not prevent him from giving absolute credit to the best man, even when that best man was black. All hail to Johnson.' London wrote that Johnson was 'superb. He was impregnable . . . as inaccessible as Mont Blanc.'

Those who defend London against charges of racism cite the letter he wrote to the Japanese-American Commercial Weekly in 1913:

In reply to yours of August 16, 1913. First of all, I should say by stopping the stupid newspaper from always fomenting race prejudice. This of course, being impossible, I would say, next, by educating the people of Japan so that they will be too intelligently tolerant to respond to any call to race prejudice. And, finally, by realizing, in industry and government, of socialism—which last word is merely a word that stands for the actual application of in the affairs of men of the theory of the Brotherhood of Man.

In the meantime the nations and races are only unruly boys who have not yet grown to the stature of men. So we must expect them to do unruly and boisterous things at times. And, just as boys grow up, so the races of mankind will grow up and laugh when they look back upon their childish quarrels.

In 1996, after the City of Whitehorse, Yukon, renamed a street in honor of London, protests over London's alleged racism forced the city to change the name of "Jack London Boulevard" back to "Two-mile Hill".

Works

Short stories

Western writer and historian Dale L. Walker writes:

London's true métier was the short story ... London's true genius lay in the short form, 7,500 words and under, where the flood of images in his teeming brain and the innate power of his narrative gift were at once constrained and freed. His stories that run longer than the magic 7,500 generally—but certainly not always—could have benefited from self-editing.

London's "strength of utterance" is at its height in his stories, and they are painstakingly well-constructed. "To Build a Fire" is the best known of all his stories. Set in the harsh Klondike, it recounts the haphazard trek of a new arrival who has ignored an old-timer's warning about the risks of traveling alone. Falling through the ice into a creek in seventy-five-below weather, the unnamed man is keenly aware that survival depends on his untested skills at quickly building a fire to dry his clothes and warm his extremities. After publishing a tame version of this story—with a sunny outcome—in The Youth's Companion in 1902, London offered a second, more severe take on the man's predicament in The Century Magazine in 1908. Reading both provides an illustration of London's growth and maturation as a writer. As Labor (1994) observes: "To compare the two versions is itself an instructive lesson in what distinguished a great work of literary art from a good children's story."

Other stories from the Klondike period include: "All Gold Canyon", about a battle between a gold prospector and a claim jumper; "The Law of Life", about an aging American Indian man abandoned by his tribe and left to die; "Love of Life", about a trek by a prospector across the Canadian tundra; "To the Man on Trail," which tells the story of a prospector fleeing the Mounted Police in a sled race, and raises the question of the contrast between written law and morality; and "An Odyssey of the North," which raises questions of conditional morality, and paints a sympathetic portrait of a man of mixed White and Aleut ancestry.

London was a boxing fan and an avid amateur boxer. "A Piece of Steak" is a tale about a match between older and younger boxers. It contrasts the differing experiences of youth and age but also raises the social question of the treatment of aging workers. "The Mexican" combines boxing with a social theme, as a young Mexican endures an unfair fight and ethnic prejudice in order to earn money with which to aid the revolution.

Several of London's stories would today be classified as science fiction. "The Unparalleled Invasion" describes germ warfare against China; "Goliath" is about an irresistible energy weapon; "The Shadow and the Flash" is a tale about two brothers who take different routes to achieving invisibility; "A Relic of the Pliocene" is a tall tale about an encounter of a modern-day man with a mammoth. "The Red One" is a late story from a period when London was intrigued by the theories of the psychiatrist and writer Jung. It tells of an island tribe held in thrall by an extraterrestrial object.

Some nineteen original collections of short stories were published during London's brief life or shortly after his death. There have been several posthumous anthologies drawn from this pool of stories. Many of these stories were located in the Klondike and the Pacific. A collection of Jack London's San Francisco Stories was published in October 2010 by Sydney Samizdat Press.

Novels

London's most famous novels are The Call of the Wild, White Fang, The Sea-Wolf, The Iron Heel, and Martin Eden.

In a letter dated Dec 27, 1901, London's Macmillan publisher George

Platt Brett, Sr., said "he believed Jack's fiction represented 'the very best kind of work' done in America."

Critic Maxwell Geismar called The Call of the Wild "a beautiful prose poem"; editor Franklin Walker said that it "belongs on a shelf with Walden and Huckleberry Finn"; and novelist E.L. Doctorow called it "a mordant parable ... his masterpiece."

The historian Dale L. Walker commented:

Jack London was an uncomfortable novelist, that form too long for his natural impatience and the quickness of his mind. His novels, even the best of them, are hugely flawed.

Some critics have said that his novels are episodic and resemble linked short stories. Dale L. Walker writes:

The Star Rover, that magnificent experiment, is actually a series of short stories connected by a unifying device ... Smoke Bellew is a series of stories bound together in a novel-like form by their reappearing protagonist, Kit Bellew; and John Barleycorn ... is a synoptic series of short episodes.

Ambrose Bierce said of The Sea-Wolf that "the great thing—and it is among the greatest of things—is that tremendous creation, Wolf Larsen ... the hewing out and setting up of such a figure is enough for a man to do in one lifetime." However, he noted, "The love element, with its absurd suppressions, and impossible proprieties, is awful."

The Iron Heel is interesting as an example of a dystopian novel that anticipates and influenced George Orwell's Nineteen Eighty-Four. London's socialist politics are explicitly on display here. The Iron Heel meets the contemporary definition of soft science fiction. The Star Rover (1915) is also science fiction.

Apocrypha

Jack London Credo

110

London's literary executor, Irving Shepard, quoted a Jack London Credo in an introduction to a 1956 collection of London stories:

I would rather be ashes than dust!

I would rather that my spark should burn out in a brilliant blaze than it should be stifled by dry-rot.

I would rather be a superb meteor, every atom of me in magnificent glow, than a sleepy and permanent planet.

The function of man is to live, not to exist.

I shall not waste my days in trying to prolong them.

I shall use my time.

The biographer Stasz notes that the passage "has many marks of London's style" but the only line that could be safely attributed to London was the first. The words Shepard quoted were from a story in the San Francisco Bulletin, December 2, 1916, by journalist Ernest J. Hopkins, who visited the ranch just weeks before London's death. Stasz notes, "Even more so than today journalists' quotes were unreliable or even sheer inventions," and says no direct source in London's writings has been found. However, at least one line, according to Stasz, is authentic, being referenced by London and written in his own hand in the autograph book of Australian suffragette Vida Goldstein:

Dear Miss Goldstein:–

Seven years ago I wrote you that I'd rather be ashes than dust. I still subscribe to that sentiment.

Sincerely yours,

Jack London

Jan. 13, 1909

Furthermore, in his short story "By The Turtles of Tasman", a character, defending her ne'er-do-well grasshopperish father to her antlike uncle, says: "... my father has been a king. He has lived .... Have you lived merely to live? Are you afraid to die? I'd rather sing one wild song and burst my heart with it, than live a thousand years watching my digestion and being afraid of the wet. When you are dust, my father will be ashes."

"The Scab"

A short diatribe on "The Scab" is often quoted within the U.S. labor movement and frequently attributed to London. It opens:

After God had finished the rattlesnake, the toad, and the vampire, he had some awful substance left with which he made a scab. A scab is a two-legged animal with a corkscrew soul, a water brain, a combination backbone of jelly and glue. Where others have hearts, he carries a tumor of rotten principles. When a scab comes down the street, men turn their backs and Angels weep in Heaven, and the Devil shuts the gates of hell to keep him out....

In 1913 and 1914, a number of newspapers printed the first three sentences with varying terms used instead of "scab", such as "knocker", "stool pigeon" or "scandal monger".

This passage as given above was the subject of a 1974 Supreme Court case, Letter Carriers v. Austin, in which Justice Thurgood Marshall referred to it as "a well-known piece of trade union literature, generally attributed to author Jack London". A union newsletter had published a "list of scabs," which was granted to be factual and therefore not libelous, but then went on to quote the passage as the "definition of a scab". The case turned on the question of whether the "definition" was defamatory. The court ruled that "Jack London's... 'definition of a scab' is merely rhetorical hyperbole, a lusty and imaginative expression of the contempt felt by union members towards those who refuse to join", and as such was not libelous and was protected under the First Amendment.

Despite being frequently attributed to London, the passage does not appear at all in the extensive collection of his writings at Sonoma State University's website. However, in his book The War of the Classes he published a 1903 speech entitled "The Scab", which gave a much more balanced view of the topic:

The laborer who gives more time or strength or skill for the same wage than another, or equal time or strength or skill for a less wage, is a scab. The generousness on his part is hurtful to his fellow-laborers, for it compels them to an equal generousness which is not to their liking, and which gives them less of food and shelter. But a word may be said for the scab. Just as his act makes his rivals compulsorily generous, so do they, by fortune of birth and training, make compulsory his act of generousness.

[...]

Nobody desires to scab, to give most for least. The ambition of every individual is quite the opposite, to give least for most; and, as a result, living in a tooth-and-nail society, battle royal is waged by the ambitious individuals. But in its most salient aspect, that of the struggle over the division of the joint product, it is no longer a battle between individuals, but between groups of individuals. Capital and labor apply themselves to raw material, make something useful out of it, add to its value, and then proceed to quarrel over the division of the added value. Neither cares to give most for least. Each is intent on giving less than the other and on receiving more. (Source: Wikipedia)

CPSIA information can be obtained
at www.ICGtesting.com
Printed in the USA
BVHW031118100719
553058BV00007B/205/P